MR WRONG

A NOVEL BY LINDSEY DAVIES

Whiteley Publishing

Published by Whiteley Publishing Ltd
First paperback edition 2013

ISBN 978-1-908586-51-3

Special Thanks and Dedications

I would sincerely like to thank certain people in my life who have been whole-heartedly supportive whilst maintaining faith, even through my darkest hours.

Firstly there's my family: Enormous thanks and love to my Dad Glyn and his wife Karen for complete support, financial assistance and caring for my children whilst I pursue my dreams. Special thanks and love to my mother Barbara and husband Peter for persisting and contributing consistently in numerous ways. My Grandparents, Bernard and Irene who are loved dearly and I thank you for your complete faith and support throughout my turbulent life. Lastly, I would like to thank Linda and husband Tony, whom I consider my family and I am blessed to have you in my life.

Friends: It cannot be said strongly enough how grateful and appreciative I am to my best friend Helen. A friend who has never given up on me and has been there through every situation in my life and has proved the upmost loyalty – you're like a sister to me. Massive thanks to my oldest friend Tony who has endured every boyfriend discussion and offered the sincerest advice and support. Michelle, Tania, Jo and Gill, and Gareth – your support has been immense.

Comedians: To all my friends on the comedy circuit, who have offered invaluable advice, support and have faith in my material. Special mentions: Nina Gilligan, Freddy Quinne, Dave Twentyman, Kenny Mills, Bobby Murdock, Lewis Charlesworth, Lee Thomasson and Carl Lawrence whom I consider friends and I thank you eternally for your advice regarding comedy and self- improvement.

Final Thanks: The most important thank you of them all – my dear children. We've had a rough few years and I thank you for your perseverance. I persist for you solely to give you the best opportunities in life. Alex, Adrienne and Grace, I love you with all my heart.

Contents

Chapter 1

The Truth

Any woman with experience will know only too well the cause of all problems... MEN! It really makes no difference whether we are sad, depressed, neglected, betrayed or simply pissed off – men are the root of every bad emotion a woman dreads to feel. So, why is it that we persist in having the life, hope and dignity sucked out of us by falling in love over and over again? Why, after every failed relationship are we convinced that the next one will be the one?

I have had my fair share of unsuccessful relationships and the giant boot of man has trodden on my head so many times that I have become accustomed to the repetitive tramping so much, that I expect it. I am a self confessed pessimist who has learned that Prince Charming, Mr Right or even the Average Joe does not exist! In twenty years I have tried on so many pairs of trousers that I have struggled to find a pair that fits. Not that I need them to fit perfectly. I can wear a pair that's a little loose or short in the leg, but the ones I try on? Well, I can say with experience that they either fall down or won't pull up past the thighs. The Lycra ones fit perfectly but they aren't a heterosexual fitting.

Through past experiences I have learned to be very selective when seeking out a new, worse half. I don't expect him to succumb to my every need but I believe that I deserve a half decent half wit who doesn't lie, cheat, steal, moan, piss on my bathroom floor or belittle everything I do or say. There are only so many bottles of bathroom cleaner I can stomach before I eventually snap. How many pairs of socks does it take to pick up from your bedroom floor before you succumb to psycho tendencies? These days, it takes just one pair, one pair of sweaty, toe holed socks before I pack his belongings and show him the window.

Being single has its ups and downs, but personally I prefer the in and out aspect of that status. I'm handling it really well since Marcus and I separated. You really do know when your heart gets broken. You're not just upset, you're a communicative nightmare. Friends gathered round on a daily basis to console me or get me pissed but I knew deep down they wanted to shout, 'Shut the fuck up, Roxy! Get a fucking grip!' They never did say that because they are my friends. I did appreciate the free wine though. I think I prolonged my grievances just to expose their generosity. I'd had break ups in the past, got a little teary and superimposed my ex's face to my toilet roll, but with Marcus I had snot bubbles and eyes that would make Satan himself proud. I would have to finger my own face to aid a smile and sure, it took two hundred boxes of tissues, approximately one hundred and twenty two tubs of ice cream and sex with many to move forward but it was over and there was nothing I could do to change that. I could either dry up or live it up and I was very much a latter type of woman. In hindsight, I realised that there were too many negatives in our relationship that couldn't be repaired. There was a serious lack of communication. He said to me once, 'actions speak louder than words,' so I punched him in the face. Not a good end to the relationship really but that break up lead me to a new understanding about life as a singleton in my thirties.

For the past three years I've been single and trawling the country for a suitable partner. Throughout my endeavours I have learned something that I never realised before. Every single man has that one essential flaw that you can't abide, escape or live with in matrimony or simply cohabiting. That's my observation and my opinion! My friends have partners or husbands but there's always something that they discover, something that increases the urge to hit them, so hard that a visit to Accident and Emergency is justified. I'm not talking about silly little flaws like nail biting or leaving the toilet seat up, even though I have justified a break up with both those reasons as the basis. I'm talking about real flaws, annoyances that make you run to the porn shop and live happily ever after with your inanimate pet rabbit.

I have met women who openly talk about how wonderful their husbands are and how they can want for nothing. I would listen to these creatures of disillusionment and listen to the bullshit that fall out of their misapprehended mouths. Blah! Blah! Blah! I would obtusely smile at the chosen ones and mumble 'bollocks, love' under my breath. I would go home and wonder if I was being too pessimistic and maybe there's a slight chance that I could eventually praise my other half as if they are some type of God but then I would think of my previous mishaps, pour a glass of wine and think myself lucky that I was in a position to enjoy my freedom. For a short while anyway. Eventually that longing for a partner kicks in like the need for chocolate during menstruation. That need when you are menstruating and you check every cupboard in the house for some sweet delight.

The thing is I want to settle down again and share my life with someone, but that someone has to prove me wrong. I'm not saying there aren't any decent men in the world but that I was looking in the wrong places. I can accept that everyone has faults as do I, but I needed to find someone on my wavelength, someone who understood me, someone who was well endowed. My friends say I have OCD 'Obsessive Cock Disorder' but I'm a quantity girl, always have been. Preferring the bigger package only proves that I'm not actually shallow, doesn't it?

I guess my reservations about men came from a string of disasters in my past. I was seventeen when I met my first love and I was under pressure to have sex from non-virginal friends. After I left my hymen on his mattress, I thought we would be together forever but that's what you would think when you're a newcomer. It didn't last because I learned my first lesson about men, which is 'a way to their heart is through their stomach'. Although, that wasn't my first thought when I caught him eating... my best friend! Seven months in my first sexual relationship and I was cuckolded. I remember the anger that overcame me. It wasn't a proud moment but one that still makes me smile when I remember his face when I told him I had Aids. Of course I don't have Aids and it was a very immature and vengefully cruel thing to say but for one split second I felt better. That slap in the face was the first of many but the redder my cheeks became, the stronger I grew.

I met another guy shortly after and again, I thought our love was written in the stars, turns out it wasn't. You see, I'm an Aquarian and he was a dick. I valuably learned not to be gullible in my younger years as a singleton. I naively took the advice from a friend once. I had a hot date lined up and I was terrified going back into the minefield that was singlehood. My friend advised me to go out 'dressed to kill'. He ran a fucking mile when I turned up in a balaclava, holding a machete. Not one of my finer moments I can assure you.

I pray for fate to deliver someone who isn't like the wasters I've experienced in my past. I have got myself involved with so many relationships, some short, some very short and some for one night only. Maybe the Universe is working with my negativity and that if I don't try to imagine myself with someone perfect then I'll be cursed with a life of wretched idiots. I struggle to dream about my perfect man because to be honest, I don't even know what I want. That's just me, Roxy Hart, thirty seven years of age, too old to pull off a mini skirt, but not old enough to the point that when I sneeze, I piss myself.

As an experiment and to prove to my friends as well as myself, I was going to go on a journey to prove that Mr Right is a myth. A story. A fairy tale. Reality was harsh and the dating game was becoming a game to me. It was going to be a long journey, a road of unknown possibilities. If I found a compatible companion then I would deem myself a very lucky woman, otherwise it will be an experience and first hand advice, which I can pass on to my children. I needed to get cracking then, my maternal clock was ticking, the menopause can seize me at any point. When I'm emotional and sweaty, no man will want to play my game then. I need to move fast. Who knows? Maybe I will find my happy ending.

It's a New Year and my resolution was to move on… with another prick!

Chapter 2

The Mummy's Boy

Family are a colossal part of my life. Sometimes certain members disapprove of my choices and I can tell that they are trying to hold back the vomit when they realise I have yet another new boyfriend. It doesn't matter how many bad decisions I make or however slutty I behave, they support me on a level that is expected. Normality was for me to vent my anger about my latest break up to my mother who, despite her facial expression of disappointment, absolutely lived for the gossip. I'd ring her following another loss and inform her that I would be visiting; she'd have the kettle boiling before I'd even put down the phone. She'd make sure I was comfy and lay out a tray of sugary delights just to make sure I stayed long enough to fill her in on every, morbid detail. She was living my life through her own mind, anticipating the news like a frenzied, media enthusiast.

I held no doubt that my mother was just being there for me in her own, inquisitive way and that my tales of woe were just an escape from her own problems, which I was fine with. I was fond of the cake to be honest, a break up always called for lots of cake. I am generally close with my mother, despite her neurosis that I was destined to be suffocated in my sleep by my cats, with no man to shed any tears over my feline fate. She wasn't nosey really, she just liked to spend time with me, even if it was to listen to my current, idiotic choice of boyfriend. What I'm saying is she knows when she should be there for me. I'm not smothered, mithered or wrapped in fleece. She's available when I need her and that's what I think a mother should be like once we are set free from the nest. Looking at my life since leaving home, I may have left the nest but I certainly wasn't catching the best worms.

The day I encountered Matt Shelvin, I was food shopping in the local supermarket. I was browsing the vegetable section and emulating masturbation with a cucumber to show off in front of my best friend, Helen. I caught him laughing to himself stood near the lettuces and being who I am, I proceeded to walk over to try and explain my immature behaviour.

'Sorry about that, I'm just dicking around with my friend.' I realised I was still holding the cucumber. The shopper looked casually delightful in his shorts and polo shirt. His brown hair swept to one side was an alluring feature, which was almost regal looking. I was used to the shaven type. Not because they chose to look like a thug, but because they had no choice due to poor hereditary hair lines. Whilst looking at him I felt concern for my wellbeing as I seem to be attracted to most men who smile at me. I convinced myself in a matter of seconds that it was purely coincidental and fate was my friend. I looked hopeful as he responded.

'It's fine. I was thinking about putting your cucumber and my lettuce together.' He smiled and held up the lettuce. I felt the redness in my face and I must have looked ridiculous next to the cucumber, red and green look terrible together. I needed a retort and fast.

'Your lettuce appears too dry for my cucumber. Actually this is weird.' I paused in a train of thought. He seemed agreeable.

'I suppose this innuendo is a little childish.' He replied. I was looking at his lettuce and then at my cucumber, then it hit me.

'That's what's weird. Here, you take the cucumber and I'll have the lettuce. That's much more appropriate. Now the gender is right.' I could tell from his cringe worthy expression that I had taken vegetable innuendo a tad too far. He started to look past my head with puzzlement. I turned around to see Helen admiring herself in an overhead mirror, holding a pair of melons up against her breasts. 'Oh God, sorry about her, she's easily amused.' An introduction was needed to intercept the ongoing embarrassment. 'I'm Roxy by the way.'

'Hi, I'm Matt and I don't generally use phallicism with vegetables... unless, I'm influenced by a beautiful woman.'

'Well, I do because I'm clearly that childish.' I don't think my response was desirable but his smile reflected his amusement by my honesty. Helen was approaching with the trolley, packed with our weekend essentials such as wine, crisps, dips and the latest rom com releases. Matt was staring into the trolley.

'So, what's a couple of lovely single ladies like yourselves doing this weekend? Looks like a quiet night in.' Matt was an observational genius.

'Oh, I'm not single. I'm a married woman. Ten years in fact. This is Roxy's shopping, its standard for the weekend,' explained Helen. I could have hit her in the face with the lettuce. Great, now he thinks I'm some kind of sad, crazy lady who sits in at the weekends watching DVD's, pissed and stuffing my face desperately hoping that the lead guy from the movie will come knocking on my door and ravage me intensely over the back of the couch. OK, he'd be right but I didn't need my best friend illuminating the scenario.

'Ha Ha, Helen, don't be stupid.' I turned to Matt. 'She always tries to show me up in public, don't you, Helen?'

'No,' replied Helen sternly. Helen was too serious for her own good sometimes. After twenty years of friendship, you'd think she understood me. Not many people do.

'Yes but we take it in turns, don't we? Like a game?' I was getting anxious and thought about cracking a bottle of the wine right there, on the supermarket floor. I envisaged a drunken scenario, pissed out of my head as Helen ran around the supermarket with me in the trolley, legs akimbo, singing some heavy metal song containing the words 'mother fucker'. A little far fetched but that was the level of humiliation I was feeling as Matt maintained a stretched smile.

'It's nice that you choose to spend your weekends finding yourself. Most girls are out every weekend, drinking themselves stupid, shouting obscenities and pissing behind the nearest skip. It's alluring that you don't conform to that lifestyle.' Matt seemed impressed. Helen erupted with laughter.

'Ha Ha, you've just described...' Helen suddenly stopped speaking as the trolley steered itself into the back of her ankles. It seems that she does know me after all but I don't want a new potential date to know that, not till at least the third date.

'So, you are single then?' Asked Matt confidently. He seemed hopeful and I had nothing to lose but my dignity again and that was becoming a regular occurrence.

'Yes, yes I am.' I was secretly enjoying the flattery. Being asked out is a wonderful feeling – unless it's by a seventy old man in a flat cap who doesn't even notice the colour of my eyes. I was confident about Matt because I was wearing a high neckline.

Matt opened his wallet and passed me a business card. 'Here, my number is on there. If you don't like the movie this weekend, feel free to give me a ring and I'll gladly take you out.' Helen was elbowing me in the arm, grinning and basically leaving me with no choice even if he had a face like Michael Winner. She always got enthusiastic every time there was a potential husband on the scene. She was one of the few lucky ones who had a husband who doted on her completely. She wore the trousers and he wore suspenders – in the bedroom of course. She was a nymphomaniac and not afraid to fill me in all the morbid details of their passionate, albeit weird sex life. I admired her for her upfront approach to sex. I just wish she didn't tell me every time I was eating.

I took the card from Matt and read the card. I think he gave me the card to show off his contract cleaning business. The card read 'Spick n Span'. A man with a cleaning company. Matt was either both entrepreneurial and found a niche in the market or he was just another misogynistic twat with an ego. Only one way to find out, I thought.

'Thanks, maybe I'll ring you... this Friday night, about eight o clock.' The desperation dripped out of every orifice. My mother always tells me to think before I speak but I forget every time I do speak. Maybe there's a medication for it – it would complement the Citalopram. I stared at Matt and gave him by best flirtatious eyes, hoping that it would create some distance from my needy reply. He was just about to say something and his phone rang. He answered it so fast, he almost dropped his phone. Helen and I stood there, loitering like a couple of nosey, busy bodies. We could have just walked off but it would be rude not to say goodbye at least.

'Hi, Mummy. Yes, I'm just picking up your bath salts...' said Matt. Helen and I looked at one another, both of us forcefully trying not to grin in Matt's face over 'mummy'. Helen's partial grin was making me want to erupt with laughter so I started to read the back of one of the DVD's to look occupied and less bitchy – Helen continued to grin.

'Lunch sounds lovely, Mummy. I'll be round at one. See you later... love you too. Bye bye.' Matt put down the phone and didn't seem fazed by his conversation with Mummy. 'Sorry about that,' said Matt, 'that was my Mother.'

'Really, I wouldn't have guessed.' Helen received another jab in the ankles. I needed to counteract her sarcastic riposte.

'I'm always picking stuff up for my Mummy.' That should do it, I thought. Matt's remaining smile stayed so I thought it would be a good time to leave before Helen or I put our heels in it again. 'Well, it's lovely to meet you, Matt. I'll speak to you Friday, I guess.'

'I'll wait for your call.' Replied Matt. I grabbed the trolley and Helen's arm and headed straight for the tills. Helen kept looking back at Matt.

'What are you dragging me away for?' Asked Helen. I had to wait till we were completely out of sight before I responded.

'I've told you before. You're not allowed to speak when I'm conversing with men. You made me sound like a right skank. I do not piss in public!' Helen knew I was lecturing more than being angry.

'You did take a piss behind that skip once. Remember, it was the night we missed the last bus and you had to use the napkin from the kebab to wipe yourself.' Helen was too honest for her own good sometimes, but sadly, she was right about that night. I hate it when she remembers drunken nights out. I drink copious amounts to avoid morning after flashbacks. Helen isn't a very good drunk so she limits herself to five glasses. Any more than that and she's shouting 'penis' at the top of her voice and flashing her knickers to any man that will take notice. She loves married life but after a few drinks I think she's reminded of how she missed out on the single life and acts a little rebellious. Helen has witnessed some of my disastrous escapades. I'm positive she's thankful that her husband Scott is the only man who'll ever make her happy. I envy her sometimes. She's allowed to go out whenever she likes and receives complete trust from her husband. He works really hard and still manages to share the housework and cooking. If I had to find a flaw in Scott it would be his inability to laugh. He's a doting husband who makes my friend happy but he's inherently boring. I've never met someone so serious. I'm not convinced he even likes me but he conceals it well – I can tell by his expressionless face.

Helen and I unload our groceries onto the belt and I'm packing like a girl guide trying to raise money for charity. I didn't want Matt to catch up with us – I needed a couple of days to overcome the embarrassment of our initial meeting. By Friday, I would have consumed a couple of glasses of wine – I like to call it confidence in a glass.

We are driving home and Helen hasn't spoken for five minutes and twenty five seconds. I often time this when it happens because it's such a rarity. The record so far is six minutes twelve seconds. That was when she'd had a filling at the Dentist though. I looked at my watch as six minutes approached. Five minutes, forty two. That was close.

'So, are you going to ring him then?' Asked Helen.

'Yes, on Friday, like I said I would.' I was actually looking forward to it. 'Did you think I was fobbing him off?' Helen stopped at the traffic lights.

'No, but I never know when you're being serious or not.' Helen started to smirk. 'And besides, it depends if he's got plans with Mummy.' We both erupted with laughter. Helen always liked to break the ice with things, she hated ay tension between us. We were more like squabbling sisters than friends. The closeness was comforting as I had no other siblings.

Friday night had arrived and I was on my second glass of wine. I'd rang Matt earlier and arranged a time and place. The venue was a nice little bar, which was quiet enough to talk. There's nothing worse than a first date in a noisy nightclub surrounded by hen parties chanting 'I'm getting married in the morning'. Like I need that shit rubbing in my face on a first date. I wouldn't want him to see my bitter face so early on. I also opted out of the cinema when Matt suggested it on the phone. How the hell can you get to know somebody when it's dark, you can't speak and other couples are cuddling up together? I don't like awkward situations and I'll avoid them at all costs, even if

I do create most of them unwittingly.

I arrived at the bar and Matt was sitting in the corner. He was dressed smartly and I was impressed how he rose from his chair as I arrived. Manners are important and should be used daily, in every situation. Well mannered people are admired and respected, more words of wisdom from my mother. I sat down at the table.

'Hello again, Matt, am I late?' I was sure I wasn't.

'No, not at all. I've only been here a few minutes.' Matt gestured to the waiter who walked over to our table. 'Hi, could we have the menu please?' The waiter smiled and passed over the menus.

'Certainly, Sir, may I recommend the sea bass?' Said the waiter. I looked at the table and noticed that it was set for three people. The waiter also left a third menu on the table. I was hoping Matt didn't have an imaginary friend or some kind of schizophrenic ailment. I looked up and saw an elder woman, in her fifties at a guess, walking up to the table. She was looking me up and down, strangely paying more attention to me than my date. I stood up as she approached the table.

'Now now, there's no need to rise, I'm not royalty,' explained the woman. She sat down beside me, I knew what was coming. Matt spoke.

'Roxy, this is my mother, Delilah. You don't mind if she joins us do you?' Like I had a choice. I wasn't sure whether to run and hide or stay out of sheer, morbid curiosity. I considered the situation quickly and reached the conclusion that if she approved of me then maybe she'd allow me to have some private time with her handsome son. This was the closest I'd ever got to engaging in a threesome – just not the threesome I have when watching Gerard Butler and Bradley Cooper on DVD. This was going to be a new experience and one for the girls so I decided to assume my position and go ahead with this farcical date. I reached out my hand to Delilah.

'Lovely to meet you, Delilah.' I'm sure my grip was too harsh; it must have been the nerves. I noticed that Delilah was wearing a wedding ring. 'Will your husband be joining us tonight?' Delilah let go of my hand and I looked at Matt who was widening his eyes and shaking his head slightly.

'My husband died last year, so no, he won't be joining us,' Replied Delilah sternly. Great start, I thought. I've insulted Mummy and I've not even ordered from the menu. I envisaged a night of awkward moments. I needed a drink and fast. The waiter was hovering at the table.

'Could I order a large glass of white wine, please?' I asked in a formal tone to win back some points. Delilah stopped staring at me long enough to order a drink.

'I'll have a glass of soda water please and a glass of orange juice,' ordered Delilah. She spoke in a very stern tone, one which was quite terrifying. I was confused about her order, Matt was silent.

'You must be thirsty, Delilah?' I was given a look so stern that I imagined snakes hissing at me upon her head. Medusa continued to fixate her concrete expression.

'The orange is for Matthew. He doesn't like to drink. Do you, Matthew?' Delilah turned her stone like face into a smile towards her son. My date!

'No, Mummy,' replied Matt. I was astonished by Matt's silence. He didn't seem the confident man I met in the Supermarket. Maybe I should have brought a cucumber to bring his out of his shell. I froze for a moment as Delilah stood up.

'I'm just going to the ladies room, shan't be long, Matthew. Would you order the chicken salad for me?' Asked Delilah.

'Yes, of course.' Matt was smiling more. 'See you in a minute.'

Delilah walked round the table to Matt, grabbed his face and kissed him on the lips like he was a ten year old boy on his birthday. 'Thank you, my darling.' She walked towards the toilets. Matt released an enormous sigh.

'I'm so sorry about his. Mummy insisted on coming along. It's been so long since my last girlfriend, she wanted to make sure I'd made a good choice.' Matt suddenly perked up. He smiled at me and reached across the table to hold my hand. I'd known him five minutes and he wanted to hold my hand already. This seemed a little bit strange but I assumed that his mummy has raised him with old fashioned values. He looked quite sweet, especially when he gestured the waiter to come over. There was a hint that he had a dominant side and it could only be unleashed when his mother wasn't wiping his arse alongside him. I knew within seconds that I had to get him alone to find out who he really was. I had to ditch the mother. The waiter arrived with our drinks, ready to take our orders. I perused the menu quickly.

'I'll have the chicken in white wine sauce, please.' I checked there was no garlic. Matt passed his menu back to the waiter.

'I'll have the gammon, please. And, could I order a chicken salad, without pepper? Make sure there's no pepper. Mummy has a slight allergy to pepper.' The waiter expressed the same grin as Helen and I when we first heard Matt use the word 'Mummy'. I was glad I wasn't the only judgemental one. The waiter took the menus and walked away. I'm sure I could see his shoulders quivering as he left trying not to guffaw. I probably had less than two minutes to speak with Matt before Medusa returned.

'Do you want to go somewhere else once we've finished our meals?' I asked. Matt appeared hopeful and turned to check if his mother was walking back.

'I'd love to but I have to take Mummy home.' Matt conveyed disappointment in his tone. 'It would be nice though. I don't want to hurt Mummy's feelings.' I was ready to leave without food but I felt sorry for him. He was held in purgatory by his own mother.

He was like a tiny bird with a broken wing, never unable to leave the nest. I was hoping to repair his wing and set him free and then he could visit my nest. More so, I think it was about time he tried a fresh nipple. He gazed into my eyes. 'You look stunning by the way.' Matt rubbed my hand. There was a moment of movie type romance, which I craved, despite my pessimism toward the opposite sex. I was still a girl at heart and dreamed of ever after. As I imagined a scene with Matt and I lying on the grass, wrapped in each other's arms I saw Delilah walking back to the table. The scene continued to run in my mind but a swarm of bees appeared and chased me off the field.

'Have you ordered my chicken salad, Matthew?' Asked Delilah. Matthew nodded. Delilah took a sip of her water and glanced at my glass of wine, which only had a couple of mouthfuls left. I acknowledged another Medusa glance. I hated this woman. Who was she to judge me on the pace I drink a glass of wine? If she wasn't so intimidating, I would have had three mouthfuls left. I just wished she'd stop staring and fuck off! She turned her body round towards me. 'So, Roxy, do you work at all?' I was hating this date more and more.

'I do work actually. I'm a Marketing Coordinator for a very reputable advertising agency in town.' I wasn't lying but I still felt that I needed to impress her, for Matt's sake especially.

'Do you have children, Roxy?' Enquired Delilah. I didn't have the guts to explain that my maternal clock needed batteries. The thought of children, labour and stretch marks gave me nightmares.

'No, I don't have children but I hope to have a family one day.' I think that was the correct answer. Suddenly, Delilah articulated a smile.

'Career first. That's very mature planning, Roxy. Matthew wants to start a family. I've wanted a grandchild for years.' Delilah unexpectedly became polite from the sheer prospect of grandchildren. She clearly thought that I would be the one to produce her grandchild. I wanted to scream out that this was a first date and I have no intentions of being seeded, especially by a spineless, albeit cute guy who brings his mother along on a date. I imagined she'd insist on being at the conception. Our food was placed on the table by the waiter, who was still grinning and I'd suddenly lost my appetite. Delilah was a controlling, manipulative bint with a serious Freudian way of thinking. I wanted to teach her a lesson. I'm not a vengeful woman but she was pissing me off to an extreme level. Delilah got up with a napkin and began to wipe the side of Matt's mouth. I couldn't take anymore, so I waited till her back was turned and peppered her salad. I smiled at Matt, stood up and left the bar. I decided to ignore my mother's advice on using good manners in every situation. Sometimes rudeness is necessary.

I never rang Matt after that night. It was one date with a shimmer of romance. No matter how much I liked him, he would always be a mummy's boy. I rang my mother and said that I insisted on her slapping me across the face if I ever referred to her as 'Mummy'. The experience gave Helen something to laugh at though. She lived for my post date tales. Matt was another lovely man with that essential flaw that terminates my future happiness. I wasn't fazed by the experience though; I planned to continue my plight. Mr Right doesn't exist but I was hoping that Mr Wrong could prove me wrong.

Chapter 3

The Player

Most of the men I'd flirted with or dated all gave the impression that they were primarily interested and I took that as a good sign. If someone likes you from the off and you have that initial spark then you have already laid a great foundation for a possible relationship. I'd been on quite a few dates since Marcus and I was tallying up quite a long list of unsuccessful meetings to verify that Mr Right was a myth.

Throughout my single adventures I learned one very valuable lesson; don't be a sap for talk! Another lesson noted; when a man says he wants to be friends, he actually thinks you're ugly or your vagina isn't instantly accessible. One bonehead left me feeling like a complete and utter fool. It's not often I misjudge someone's character, I regard myself as very astute and aware, it's such qualities that have guided me thus far and I was very proficient at distinguishing the substandard, probable partner.

Introducing Reece Evans. He was a tall, handsome and a very successful property developer. His portfolio was almost as impressive as his face. His face, perfectly chiselled like a roman statue, like Michael Angelo but with a bigger cock.

Reece was one of my first dates after Marcus. The thought of dating felt like a life changing interview, I was so nervous each time though, instead of dressing conservatively, I dressed like a slut. It was a meat market out there; you have to be top cow to get noticed in Single Town. Reece Evans. What can I say? He walked into the Dog and Cart one night when I was chilling out with a bottle of wine, discussing my last sexual disaster with Helen. I remember stopping in mid conversation (the juicy bit) when Reece entered the pub with his less attractive friend.

My jaw was hanging open and Helen nudged me to grab my attention... I'd lost my train of thought and was presupposing new positions for the Karma Sutra in my head.

'Hey!' Helen grabbed my arm. I turned, jaw still open. 'Have you had a stroke?' I forced my head to face her and closed my mouth quickly as I soon realised that saliva was actually seeping out of the corners.

'Sorry, Hels, I slipped off there for a minute.' I was trying to see him in peripheral vision but it wasn't enough to rerun the mini porn that was running in my head.

'What are you staring at?' Helen turned to see what was distracting me from telling her some juicy gossip.

'You see?' I grabbed Helen's arm and tried to distract her from imitating my previous manner.

'Holy Mother... he's got to be genetically modified. Men don't look like that in real life do they?' Helen turned back to face me. 'Do they?'

'No, Helen I don't think they do, it must be some kind of genetic experiment. I reckon they've borrowed genes from Brad Pitt and Johnny Depp to create that. What a fucking specimen he is.'

His smouldering looks and electric blue eyes could hypnotise any woman within view of his face. His hair was jet black in the style of a short mohawk, each strand perfectly sculptured into place. He was a snappy dresser, wearing a designer suit which complemented his bold, coloured shirt. A tie wasn't necessary for him, he perfected his look with his top two buttons unfastened to tease every female who were lucky enough to cross his path.

'Are you going to ask him out then?' Helen seemed confident and I accepted that as a major compliment. 'You could pull him you know; he'd be great for your venture.' Helen was very positive about it too, I felt awesome.

'Fuck the venture, he's a keeper.' My search for the perfect man was over; he couldn't possibly be an arsehole. He looked too good. Besides, in my head my values had smashed through the pub windows and I was envisioning he and I lying in a field of daises, no poetry, just plain old shagging! I snapped out of it quickly.

'He's probably got a matching clone made from Angelina Jolie and Halle Berry, I've no chance.' I was feeling insecure again.

'Angelina Jolie looks like a moose. He's not seen you yet. Get your fucking arse into the toilets, roll up your skirt, show off those great legs and put the lip gloss on thickly.' Helen can be very pushy sometimes, but in this instance, I thought I'd listen to her demands.

'Right, make a distraction while I nip off.' I grabbed my bag. It was crucial that he didn't notice me till I had spruced myself up; otherwise he would have known it was for his benefit. As beautiful, breathtaking and shaggable he was I refused to massage his ego.

'Distraction? How?' Helen was looking around as if something was going to happen to save her the job of being my decoy. My perfect man was standing tall, receiving his drink from the barman, his friend was looking over.

'Shit! I'm off.' I started to rush towards the toilet door. I turned round to see Helen unfasten her top buttons so her bra was visible. She stood up and walked past the men. I was already at the toilets, her licentious display wasn't necessary now. I looked on as both men smiled and their eyes followed Helen's breasts. She was strutting like a catwalk bitch and absolutely loving it. Personally, I was getting slightly pissed off, there was no need for her to do it now, I'm the one who's supposed to be catching his eye. Thank fuck she was married and very faithful.

I stood facing the toilet mirror and wiped the smudges of eyeliner under my eyelids. Reapplication was essential in this case, so was blusher, eye shadow and thick layers of lip gloss. I rolled up my skirt a good three times and unfastened my top buttons. I'm not as busty as Helen but over the past couple of months I learned to buy smaller bras to push up what cleavage I had. My B cup was transformed into a C, plus a bit of bronzer brushed in between always assists the presentation of a damn good pair of tits.

The toilet door closed behind me and I noticed that Helen wasn't sitting at our table. I looked towards the bar and there she was, flicking her hair, chatting away like a hormonal teen. This is not the Helen I know now. She used to be the worst flirt I knew and she'd only had two glasses. Scott changed her life but I'm positive she secretly wishes that she could turn back the clock and enjoy the single life. I had never seen her like this since meeting Scott, her wonderful, loving husband who lets her do what she wants and uses his bank card to do it. I was shocked but amused also. Maybe she'd had more wine than I thought? Either way, I had to walk over and find out what was going on... very fucking impressed with her assistance though, now I had to go and talk to him.

I strutted to the bar smiling at full potential, chest out and head up. Helen smiled and beckoned me over in front of the men.

'Roxy, get over here.' Helen was beaming knowing full well that she'd actually organised the meeting. I approached them, still smiling profusely.

'I wondered where you'd gone.' He turned round. 'Oh hi there, I'm Roxy.' Always professional, I reached out my hand to make his acquaintance. My throat was dry and my palms were ceaselessly sweaty. He reciprocated my gesture and had the grip of a championship wrestler. To make my anxiety worse, he stared right into my eyes. It had been a while since a man had so much of an effect that I thought I'd pissed myself, this was dangerous territory for me, my negativity towards the opposite sex were challenging me irrevocably.

'I'm Reece, Reece Evans. This here is Carl, my work colleague.' I was one lucky lady. Reece had taken his eyes away from Helen's knockers to look straight into my eyes. I had my cleavage out. What's wrong with my cleavage? To be honest, I didn't give a toss, he chose to observe me. Maybe a little too much as he took my hand and twirled me round like a jewellery box doll to check out everything what was on offer. This was a clear cut sign that he was a player but still I twirled. Any other guy did that to me I would have been insulted, thrown his drink on him and walked away. I'd become a hypocrite. He was naturally a charmer who loved the attention from women but I loved every minute. I was cast under a spell of lust for the most handsome man I'd ever laid my drunken eyes on. Helen or I never seemed to pay any attention to Carl. We'd given in to our demons and become fickle and shallow like most of the men I'd dated. It was human nature right? Giving in to a man's predatory instinct, surely for one night at least? Helen brought my wine over, which I finished effortlessly. Reece was on the ball. 'Can I buy you another?' He asked.

'Yes, thank you. I'll have another white wine, please.' I was sure that one more drink would secure at least a one night stand. Usually, I would make them wait for a few dates and earn my bedroom time but I knew deep down that men who looked like Reece could pick and choose their prey. Oh my God, I was mentally referring myself as prey. I'd become the woman I hate. The undignified!

I noticed that Helen had ditched her shallow self and had given in to speak to the lesser looking. I, on the other hand remained shallow. I turned back to Reece. 'Thanks for the drink.' Reece smiled, took my hand and kissed the back of it. I knew damn well that a man

30

who kisses a woman's hand in that way is a definite charmer. Those who over charm are those who raise the alarm. Still, I gave in and giggled like a teenage girl who'd felt the first tongue in her mouth. I acknowledged Reece's kiss. 'Oh, what was that for?' Reece looked surprised.

'How could I not kiss your hand? I hope that's a start to many more kisses.' Strangely, he seemed genuine. It had to be the wine! My confused expression or lack of self esteem was evidently obvious from Reece's expression. 'I'm being serious you know? I don't go around kissing the hands of random women.' Shit! I believed the words that were spoken from his mouth. I held a slight glimmer of hope that this gorgeous man was actually interested in me. Was he?

We spent over an hour discussing our careers and family. He seemed to be a successful property developer with a few houses under his belt. He lived alone (of course) in a luxury apartment in Manchester. He loved fishing, playing football on a Monday night and spent as much time as possible with his young daughter. It seemed that my judgement of the other gender was clouded once again. Reece was a prosperous man with a thriving business, someone who participated in outdoor activities and doted on his daughter. The saying was true. Never judge a book by it's cover. I was adamant that I was going to delve into some of his chapters.

A few weeks had gone by and I was smitten and spoiled by the wonderful, gorgeous Reece Evans. He rang me every day, text on his lunch break and surprised me with gestures of flowers and gourmet meals. Everything seemed to be going perfectly until I asked the question that makes every man wish they were still wrapped in blankets, tightly as they slept in their Moses basket. 'Where is this relationship going?'

That one single question epitomises the immaturity of man. Women have an engraved image in their head of a marriage with their special man; someone to grow old with. Someone to rest their unshaven legs over. Men view commitment like it's some type of punishment or prison sentence. Throughout a relationship they are doting, affectionate, giving and listen to every spoken word. As soon as it's suggested that the relationship should move up a level, they run and hide like a mouse in a hole. We are the cats trying to claw them out of the hole, snarling like some desperate predator, through their duped eyes anyway.

The day I spoke to Reece was when I went with him to view a potential property. It was a three bedroomed semi detached house in the City Centre. Part of me thought that he was showing me this because he was planning our future together. He'd never shown me any of his other properties before; why now? The house was built for a family. There was a large back garden, privatised by beautiful conifers, which surrounded the garden's edge. The kitchen was big enough to turn into a café and the smallest bedroom was a beautifully, decorated nursery. The master bedroom was perfect, the first room I'd seen where I could fit that sex swing I'd always wanted. I could almost taste the confetti as he lured me into each room holding my hand. After a guided tour of the house, we sat on the bench in the back garden. Reece was being more affectionate than usual, this was a good sign. As I leaned in to kiss him, we were interrupted by his mobile phone. Reece looked at the screen.

'I need to take this, it's about a mortgage. Be one tick.' He walked back into the house and I looked up at the clear sky, imagining the future. If only Marcus could see me now. He said I'd never make anything of my life but I was the type of girl to overcome negativity. Well, look at me now, penis breath. Sat outside my new, potential family home with my gorgeous, rich, Chippendale type God! Life was good.

Reece returned from his conversation and sat back down on the bench. 'I'm going to have to leave shortly, babe, I've got a meeting with the bank.' I was saddened that this moment was going to end. In hindsight, it probably wasn't the best time to ask that fatal question.

'Reece, where are we going?' There was a weird sense of relief from within me. Reece sniggered.

'Well, I'm going to drop you off back at work and I'm going to go to the bank.' I'm positive he understood my question. I'd gone so far. No point in dragging it out.

'I know that, I mean *us*. Our relationship?' I looked at Reece as I noticed perspiration kicking in on his forehead.

'Isn't this a bit too soon,' he replied. 'It's only been a month.' This was true. I wasn't asking for marriage, I just needed to know that he saw us going somewhere. I needed to know how he observed our relationship. I know from experience that a man's perspective is galaxies away from a women's viewpoint. Are women from Venus and Men from Mars? I would say no, women are from earth and men are from women!

'This isn't a proposal, Reece, don't panic.' I was panicking. 'Do you see a future for us?' I could tell from his reaction that I had completely misinterpreted the whole house tour and that he was just showing off his property. Of course he was; he'd seen my dingy little flat with two flags outside, just enough to fit the wheelie bin. By now his perspiration has turned to a quiver. It was twenty four degrees outside.

'Can we talk about this later? I really need to get to this meeting.' He stood up anxious to leave. I had no choice but to follow, I needed a lift.

As we pulled up outside work, I noticed that Reece was constantly checking his phone. How the fuck would anyone be so eager for a meeting with the bank? My former, inquisitive self had returned.

'Which bank is your meeting at?' I had to ask or it would have chipped away at my sponge like brain. 'What time is the meeting?' The normally, charming Reece had shown first signs of agitation.

'What's with all the questions?' He snapped. I left it at that. One thing I do know is that when a man becomes annoyed by a simple question, he's lying through his fucking teeth! I grabbed my bag and exited the car, slamming the door behind me. I knew from that moment that I'd been clouded by lust for the past few weeks. I needed to get to the bottom of his behaviour so I did what any rational, suspecting woman would do. Follow him. A taxi was parked up outside the office and Reece was slightly ahead at the traffic lights. In movie style fashion I jumped into the back of the taxi and asked the driver to follow the black Mercedes Sport.

We followed for about ten miles. I was panicking slightly as I counted all the money in my purse. Before the meter reached my twenty pound limit, Reece had parked up on a driveway on the outskirts of town. Call me old fashioned but I was sure that semi detached houses with driveways didn't pass for a bank. I got out of the taxi and hid behind a transit van, like some investigative journalist on the heels of a hot story. Reece was knocking at the door, I waited anxiously. A blonde woman, slender and younger than me opened the door and threw her arms around him. I set my mobile to video player. As I filmed (very shakily) I felt the bile bubbling inside of me. Reece entered Barbie's house. I carefully tip toed up the driveway and hid behind his car. I noticed he'd left the passenger window open. 'Dick head' I thought. I could just see inside the house as Barbie took off her top, revealing perfectly spherical breasts. They were about as real as my relationship with Reece. I knew it was over now. The past few weeks ran through my mind like a high speed slide show. The bile was rising and there's nothing I could do but vomit through his opened, car window. That was the first time I gained any pleasure from vomiting.

Reece Evans was a bona fide player. My first instinct was the right one. I was thrown by attractive looks and charm. It needed to happen though because it reinforced my theory that even the person you think is perfect is not! Another Mr Wrong added to my list of wankers. Reece was a charmer who thrived on his ego by keeping a string of women interested. He made Casanova seem like a virgin. I'm sure in forty years' time, he'll be sat alone, in his three bed roomed semi detached with two empty bedrooms and a nurse to change his colostomy bag. That was a vision that helped me move forward anyway.

I saw Reece a few weeks later. Typically, I was hungover and looked rough as hell. Why do you always see your ex when you look like shit? I hate that. Anyway, Reece looked right at me and walked past me like I never even existed, yet he still had a smug looking grin on his face as he walked past. He thinks he had the last laugh. He hadn't you know. I text him to tell him I'd been diagnosed with genital warts.

Chapter 4

The Geek

As I seem to spend most of my days pondering on the mishaps of my past I found myself contemplating new mistakes. Maybe I was too distrustful of the opposite sex? Maybe I was destined to be alone? I sat in my study and considered that my exhaustive job could be a problem for some men, I began to question and mentally justify possible reasons why I was single and why I only seemed to attract the ghastly types. Is it my hectic lifestyle? Are men intimidated by my assertive nature? Do they think I am a control freak? Do I look the type who is up for sex and nothing more? Am I just being too picky? I chewed the top of my pen incessantly at these ridiculous thoughts. Why do I doubt myself? I had a stream of futile relationships and my quest to prove that Mr Right is nonexistent was proving successful thus far. My meanderings didn't last long and I took the pen out of my mouth. I can't stop now, I was on a serious mission for womankind. Settling for was not an option, not for me anyway. The serial dating was fun and I was losing sincere interest in finding a life partner; the field was there to play on and I was the Captain.

Despite my gruelling work schedule I had become acclimatised to sampling an assortment of idiots but so far I had failed to correlate with someone even slightly worthy. I was confident that I wouldn't be waiting long before I found a new subject. I begrudgingly agreed with the annoying cliché that there are plenty more fish in the sea. I'd certainly had a few fish, they were slimy and left a long, lingering stench. It was strange that I was beginning to enjoy the dating scene even though I had associated with the rudest, selfish, abusive and most egotistical morons I had ever met. I think it was because my venture was proving me right – I wasn't a woman who failed and I was generally right! Besides, it wouldn't be long before I met someone else; however, it had been a while. There was no rush; I was continuously busy and there was plenty of time to get crapped on.

After a meeting at work my manager asked me to partake in some market research and investigate binge drinking. The aim was to investigate a new wine, which apparently tasted like cordial but got you completely legless. I couldn't turn this one down! The best part of this experiment was that I got to take a few bottles home to sample, which I obliged to without hesitation. I also felt it necessary to inform my superiors that free wine only encouraged binge drinking but who was I to judge the campaign?

I returned home and sat in my conservatory (glass in hand) with the bulky file handed to our company by the Client. Chapter one, Wine and the Waistline. The chapter left me feeling a little heftier once I'd read how many calories each bottle contained. I gulped as I put down the second bottle. How the hell was I going to get a date with a wine gut? Despite the vision of a fatter self I have to admit the wine was bloody tasty. I was also a little bit pissed.

Through my intoxicated state, I was still adamant on completing a spectacular report to impress my bosses. I found myself at the local library hoping I could find some physical implications of binge drinking in the medical section. I swayed through the aisles and was feeling a little giddy. I giggled at the irony of investigating binge drinking whilst wandering through the unnerving, quiet library shit faced. I could only justify my afternoon bender by assuring myself that I was only drunk through sheer professionalism and dedication to the work, which I had been assigned. I stood still for a second to allow my hazy eyes focus on the signs. There it was... Medical. I started to rummage through the health titles to put me on the right track. I moved a couple of books to one side as I sifted through the A's and was suddenly startled! There was a face peering at me through the other side.

'Shit!' I just blurted out, 'You scared the hell out of me.' Whilst stunned I inadvertently pushed one of the books off the shelf, only for it to fall on the other side and straight onto the foot of my gawker. Typically it was an encyclopaedia, amongst the paperback section.

'Aaaarghh,' Cried out the unfortunate victim. 'Watch what you're doing.'

Crap! Not only did I have to apologise to this man for my carelessness, I had to do it under the influence of an extremely high percentage wine. I tried to compose myself to the best of my capability, which wasn't currently fantastic.

'I'm so shorry, you shtartled me. Did I do any damage?' I seriously needed to sort out my speech. The screwed up face opposite me personified utter discomfort. He didn't answer! 'I really *hic* didn't mean it. I'm very shorry.'

Still no answer! I realised it was a careless move and the look he bestowed suggested that he wasn't too thrilled by my library courtesy. It wasn't deliberate; however his ignorance angered me somewhat. I made my way to where he stood.

'Hey, *hic*... I didn't mean it ok?' I received a quizzical glance. 'Are you ok?' His bewildered grin spread across his face as he looked down at his foot. I looked down too, only to find the guy was wearing wicker sandals. I mean, who the hell wears them these days? I considered the situation in my head thinking how unlucky could someone be to visit the quietest place in town wearing wicker sandals and have the heaviest book in the library fall on his foot? The alcohol infused within my blood stream took control of my emotions as I vented with laughter. Not only was I rapturous over the situation, I was slapping his back hoping he would join me in my moment of madness. Was he fuck! He screwed up his face and looked at me as if I was some kind of mentalist on day release.

'It hurt me, you know.' He actually spoke. 'I wouldn't say it was that funny... are you drunk?'

Shit, I'd been rumbled. Note for report: Never communicate with human beings after 2 bottles of wine! I looked up at him shamelessly. 'I am *hic* but it's not what you think. You see, I'm working on a report about binge drinking... *hic*... I'm just trying to be professional.' I couldn't be less professional as I looked down to see that I was still wearing my slippers. Shiiiiiiiiit!!!! I shrugged my shoulders as he noticed my foot attire. 'I guess I'm not the only one who looks like a dick.' Once more he showed no amusement by my conversation. I needed to shut up now! One thing about alcohol, it disguises as a damn good truth serum. Unfortunately it couldn't shut me up either even though I subconsciously knew not to say things out loud. The poor guy still remained though. I looked at his black, rimmed glasses and saw his blue eyes behind them. He had dark hair, unkempt and slightly grey but bestowed rugged features, which was quite pleasing to my drunken eyes. Maybe this was fate? It made a refreshing change from meeting someone who's legless and leery. Maybe he thought it was a change to meet someone who was legless and leery, he didn't look the type to venture out into the social world. What did I have to lose? I was pissed so humiliation was natural to me. I took a deep breath and smiled at the geek. 'Hey, all I need is a bottle of water and I'll be right as rain. There's a vending machine over there, would you like to sit with me? I feel a little queasy right now and don't want to be on my own. I'm sure you'd like to rest your foot?' He looked rather surprised by my suggestion.

'Oh, err... ok.' Still surprised! 'I don't usually get asked to sit with a pretty girl.' He actually produced a genuine smile. Charming I thought. It was clear that he wasn't used to female attention. This was now a challenge for me. I needed to know more about him and most importantly why he thought wicker sandals were appropriate footwear on any given day.

He walked over to the vending machine and I zigzagged my way behind him. He paid for my water, which I thought was sweet. I should have been buying his drink seeing as I probably caused a hairline fracture in his foot. Still he managed to support me to the bench outside the library, despite his own anguish.

It was warm outside and I was drinking the water like I'd been stranded on a desert for days. 'That was much needed thank you. I'm Roxy.' I thought it was about time I made a proper introduction. He reached out his hand to formally greet me.

'I'm Tony, nice to meet you.' Tony was quite shy really, he struggled to make eye contact and I was the one that was pissed. Most men would have taken advantage by now. Tony sat with his hands between his thighs like a schoolboy on his first day of high school, not knowing what the day will bring. He wasn't the type of bloke I would normally look twice at but there was a probable possibility that I had been looking in the wrong places. A bit of hair dye, a trim and a fashion lesson could turn Tony into a darn good looking chap. I was inhaling the fresh air and suddenly the bile returned. There's nothing I could do but lean over the side of the bench and release the bile. There was the essential effect of binge drinking. I'm also one of those girls who cry upon the ejaculation of vomit. Possibly the most embarrassing moment for me. Ever!

I expected Tony to get up and run but I was pleasantly surprised when he started to hold my hair back for me. That was usually a job for Helen. I grabbed a tissue out of my bag and wiped my unsightly mouth. I looked up at Tony who actually seemed genuinely concerned.

'Are you ok?' He asked. I drank what was left of the water and exhaled a large breath.

'Much better, thank you.' I was feeling like death and needed to go home and crawl into bed. 'I'm so sorry about that, I can explain.'

'It's ok, I'm just glad you're ok.' He was a sweetheart. 'Can I walk you home?' He was acting like a true gent. A rarity to say the least.

As we walked together I found out that Tony was a University graduate in biochemistry, he built computer programmes for fun and loved science fiction. I felt quite intimidated and found myself using words like 'extraordinary' just to appear half as intelligent as him. He certainly wasn't middle class but he was cleverer enough to be. I quite liked the idea of dating a brain box. Someone to help me with my case files. I did struggle to hold back the laughter when he mentioned that he was a member of Canoe Club. Who the fuck canoes these days?

Due to displaying an unforgettable first impression I insisted that Tony allow me to see him again under different circumstances. He only lived ten minutes away so it was agreed that I visit his flat and we partake in a non alcoholic evening, watching DVD's and chilling out on his sofa. Not my usual type of date but change was necessary after the last attempt at dating.

Saturday night arrived and I thought it was only fair that I put in an equal amount of effort had I been going to a club or restaurant. I didn't need to dress up too much so to make a valid effort for his sweetness at the library I went shopping and bought myself a Darth Vader t shirt. That should blow his mind, I thought. Saying that, I was caked in make up, including fake tan and false lashes. I had to put my own stamp on the look.

Upon arrival at Tony's flat I sprayed my mouth with breath freshener. It had been a few days since I'd unveiled my digestive system to Tony but I was convinced that my breath still smelled like a blocked drain. I rang the buzzer and Tony let me in. He was wearing a nice shirt and corduroy trousers, brown ones at that. I kept mentally stressing to myself that clothes do not maketh the man. To be honest though, he had brushed his hair and had shaved. I could tell because of the blood stained tissue blob on his chin. Still, he'd made an effort and I found that appealing.

I stepped into his tiny living room and I couldn't take my eyes off the walls. The room was decorated with large, old movie posters from the nineteen fifties. *The Land that Time Forgot*, *The Day the Earth Stood Still* and the original *War of the Worlds* posters were hung throughout. Not my preference but this wasn't my flat and I had no right to judge his choice of wall vomit. Tony was staring at my Darth Vader t shirt.

'Cool shirt.' He was clearly impressed. 'Which is your favourite Star Wars film?' Shit! I hadn't a fucking clue.

'Erm… the first one.' I was hopeful.

'The Phantom Menace?' He replied enthusiastically. I think my t shirt had sweat patches.

'The Phantom what?' This was another moment to prove that honesty was the best policy.

'You know,' he continued, 'the one with Darth Maul.' I could tell that he was getting a hard on just discussing it. I had to agree to avoid any further embarrassment.

'Yes, Darth Maul, that's my favourite.' When the hell did Darth Vader change his name, I thought.

Tony politely asked me to sit down on the couch and make myself comfortable. He was still showing positive signs that he was an absolute gentleman. He pointed to his coffee table.

'I'll go and make us a nice cup of tea and you can browse through my DVD's. As you're the guest, it's only fair that you choose.' Said

Tony excitedly. 'I'll not be a moment.

I saw the stack of DVD's on the table. They were a collection of films and box sets, all what seemed to be science fiction. Personally, I liked a good horror. A zombie buffet was much more appealing. I knew I should have brought some of my own. I'm hardly going to be turned on by aliens and spaceships. I barely looked at the DVD's because I was fascinated by the clutter of shit he possessed in such a tiny flat. There were ornamental figures dominating the shelves. He must have had a childish side to him because I'd ever known a grown man keep toys whilst still in his thirties. He must be lazy too, I thought because he'd not even bothered to open half of the boxes. They looked like an unwanted Christmas gift and he hadn't got round to throwing them away. Maybe he's one of those, weird hoarder types who can't let go of the simplest item?

Tony returned from the kitchen with our tea. He placed the Doctor Who tray down on the table.

'Have you picked a DVD?' I hadn't. I was too busy counting the spots on his Dalek statue. I grabbed one randomly and passed it to him. He was ecstatic. 'Excellent choice, yes!' I think he was getting overly excited. I looked at the DVD, which I was subjecting myself too. Fucking typical, I'd only bloody chosen the entire series of Babylon Five.

Three hours had gone by and I was contemplating suicide with his light saber. Not one hint of conversation was spoken. Tony was oblivious that I'd been sat there fondling my own boobs, just to try and get some attention. I had no choice but to have a sleep.

I was awoken by Tony nudging me in the arm. I woke up and wiped the saliva from the side of my mouth.

'Oh, hi.' I was so tired. 'Sorry, I must have fallen asleep.'

'You missed the final episode, it was when...' I placed my hand over Tony's mouth.

'It's ok Tony, there's no need to explain.' I'd sincerely had enough. Tony was surprised.

'Don't you want me to fill you in?' He as so eager to talk about shitty, Babylon Five. And yes, I did want him to fill me in, just not his way.

'Oh, is that the time,' I said, not even looking at my watch. I stood up and picked up my handbag. I knew this relationship wasn't going to work. Tony was a lovely man with the characteristics of an aristocrat, but fuck me, he was boring.

As I walked to the front door, I turned and noticed that Tony wasn't even that disappointed.

'We should do this again, when you're less tired.' Poor guy was deluded. I had to make a clean break.

'I don't think so, Tony. Thanks very much but this isn't for me, it's not going to work. I'm sorry.'

Tony's expression changed. 'We can try a different film, maybe The Phantom Menace, whilst it's your favourite?' Oh dear god! I didn't even reply. I got in my car and drove, a little over the thirty limit.

Another lesson learned. Even the nicest blokes have one essential flaw that makes it impossible to maintain a healthy, compatible relationship. I had a long way to go. I decided not to contact Tony again, even if it was from a galaxy far, far away.

Chapter 5

The Miser

I had placed my future in my own hands and it felt darn good too. I was content in facing my life as a strong independent woman and having the choice to have or not to have a man in tow. It even crossed my unenthusiastic mind that maybe my experiment would prove to prove me wrong. Maybe, just maybe my Prince Charming would enter my life and exceed past a few weeks at least (and I could also win the Euro lottery two weeks in a row). A few months with a man can feel like two years so I was not going to overdo it, I usually pride myself on being consistent. I suppose consistency was my strong point, I did occupy myself with one jerk after another. Call me whatever you please but you could never say that I lack consistency.

The day I met Daryl Mackintosh was when I attended an advertising campaign down in London. I had been assigned to the marketing manager. I couldn't refuse free hotel, food and wine, only an idiot would. The campaign wasn't the liveliest event I had attended but I needed the extra cash, so I vowed to endure the boredom. I had to sit in a huge convention room for hours whilst some wannabe entrepreneur rambled on about how a new soft drink would guarantee the weight loss of at least 5lbs a week. The whole presentation was a bigger deception than my past dealings with men, or maybe once again my cynical side was getting the better of me because it was a man undertaking the presentation. I surmised that if it was a woman marketing the product I would have probably clapped, cheered, ordered a year's supply and convinced myself that I was a size 6 after just a few bottles.

After a few, gruelling life-sucking hours my backside had become increasingly numb from the wooden, rickety chair I was sitting on. I decided to scan the room and check out the talent. After the presentation from hell, I mingled around the room to the best of my ability amongst the upper class, even though I felt out of place. I detested the way people referred to themselves as 'one'.

'Would one care for a shrimp?' Asked the waiter. I felt like turning round and slapping the pompous words out of his pretentious mouth. I looked over my shoulder to acknowledge the waiter. Stood before me was a demigod. He was a tall, tanned, delicious looking waiter who smiled so adoringly that I would have eaten horse manure of his tray if he offered it. I had to oblige.

'Ta very much,' I replied with my husky northern accent.

'You're Northern,' continued the delicious waiter. 'Thank Christ for that, I thought I would have to put on this ridiculous accent all day. I'm Daryl.'

Score! He wasn't a pompous swine after all, he was from my world. 'Hi. Roxy Hart. You carry off the posh, Southern accent very well, I must say. Jolly good, old chap.' We giggled as one.

'I'm a performing arts student up in Manchester so jobs like this are like role play.' He impressed me. It was good to know he wasn't afraid of role play.

'Oh,' I liked the charismatic way he integrated his talent to con the high class morons we were forced to associate with. I had to break the ice. 'So what other types of role play do you participate in?' I was a Millennium woman. I always believed that sometimes a woman had to make the first move, especially when I knew that the majority of men were gutless. I'd been hypothetically shit on enough times to know that the odd rejection meant nothing; it was a part of life.

Phew! Lucky for me he was highly amused with my cheeky banter and the fact that we lived within a few miles of one another made this case study so much easier to stomach.

We agreed to meet up in a mutual place, in a restaurant a couple of miles from my home. I was so edgy. I wasn't used to dating, especially when it meant travelling to meet someone I barely knew. Once I arrived, Daryl was stood outside with a single red rose in his hand. *Cheesey,* I thought but the gesture deserved a kiss on the cheek and a lopsided smile. If he thought that I was going to swoon and give him my flower too then he had a long way to go. I never swoon over the obvious anymore; my inexperience had left me a long time ago.

Throughout the meal, I learned that he was quite a decent bloke. He'd had his fair share of relationships, worked hard, studied hard and was driven with ambition. The fact that he laughed at my jokes made the date more relaxing. There is nothing worse than saying something that you genuinely think is funny, the silence crushes the moment and you wished you had been knocked unconscious by the tumbleweeds.

From the perspective of a first date, I'd say it went reasonably well... until his phone rang. I watched with confusion as he spoke...

'OK, OK,' He seemed worried slightly, 'I'll be there as soon as I can, don't worry.'

I felt intrusive asking but it looked serious, 'Is everything OK?' His expression wasn't exactly jovial.

'It, it's my brother; he's just been in a car accident.' He paused to take a deep breath. 'That was my mother on the phone. I'm sorry I really have to go. I'll call you tomorrow, I promise.'

'It's ok, you get yourself...' I didn't get chance to finish my sentence, he'd left so quickly I could smell the rubber from his shoes. I sat still for a while to absorb what had just happened,

'Here's your bill Madam.' FUCK! I was stuck paying for the lot. Normally I would have flipped but I suppose my date had good reason.

'Thank you,' I placed the money on the table and left at a similar speed my date did.

Apart from being penniless whilst waiting an hour for the bus in the torrential rain, the date wasn't too bad and he kept his promise and rang me the morning after. Apparently, his brother had just broken a few ribs so I didn't have to be sympathetic about someone I didn't know, there is nothing worse.

A few weeks went by and we met up a quite a few times, the thing was I saw a pattern emerging. It seemed that every time we went anywhere, either he'd forgotten his wallet, the cash machine was out of order or he'd just been mugged. I don't ever recall seeing any signs of bruising or foul play. One day I did ask him if I could borrow a few pounds for petrol, even though I was running him to college. A day later, the cheeky blighter asked for his three pounds and twenty two pence back! I was the Queen of running over the intended petrol amount. Eventually, I realized that it was I who was being mugged. This tit was nothing more than a miser. A scrounger who couldn't pay respect never mind amenities. Maybe he had a weird phobia. I don't recall him paying for anything at all. If I add up the cost of the alcohol, cigarettes and food I paid for, I was wasting half my wage on this loser. We had reached the six week mark anyway and I wasn't prepared to risk any longer with someone who would go to the lengths of faking a car crash to escape paying for something he'd eaten. Sometimes I paid for his taxi home, which basically made him a glorified gigolo. Looking back now I remember the fat bastard also had second helpings at the restaurant. Moreover, the gesture of the red rose? Obviously, the tight arsed tosser wouldn't release the moths from his wallet to pay for a full bunch. Maybe he took the rose from his imaginary dead grandmother's grave.

The day I ended the relationship was quite difficult and I had to use harsh tactics to get through to him. We met outside the college where he studied and I was prepared to do the deed. It was awkward because he looked rather pleased to see me. I began my rehearsed speech. 'Listen, I thought it would be best to tell you face to face, but I really don't see this relationship going anywhere.' I thought I was dumping him in the most appropriate way. He didn't look so thrilled at my approach. The look he conveyed was as if he had been forced to pay for a cup of coffee or something of similar price.

'Oh, this is nice isn't it, I meet you for lunch and you dump me, thanks a lot.' He brushed his hand through his hair and started to pace back and forth. 'Do I get a reason? I didn't see a problem. I'm sure we can sort this out.'

'Definitely not! I'm sorry, I've had fun but I'm not ready to take the relationship any further, I can't see it going anywhere to be honest.' I wanted to withhold the real reason to spare his feelings. He was becoming more agitated with each step.

'Fine, I wasn't planning on taking the relationship any further either.' He began to walk back towards the college entrance. 'I can do better anyway.' He was blatantly pissed off. Or was he? He was a drama student and could bullshit with the best of them. No matter which flaw a man beholds, they always predictably turn heel when their ego is deflated through being dumped by a woman. It's as if there's no equality in dumping and women should always be the dumpee instead of the dumper. Well, guess what? I am a woman all for equality and if my man cannot pay his share, wash my pots or equally share the oral sex then he can kiss my moral arse! He began to stare right at me, I could see his anger was essentially from the image of giant pound signs dancing around my feet, making the squealing sound of laughter.

'You're just a slapper anyway. Good riddance.' The ego again! Enough was enough.

'SLAPPER?' I shouted, 'Ok rent boy, the real reason I'm ending it is because your wallet is closed so tightly that even a jack hammer couldn't crack it open. You are a skinflint who needs to start coughing up money instead of bullshit. Good day!'

I walked away feeling better for telling him the truth and I believe the other reason he turned foul was that I did not end up paying for lunch. He was another product of evidence that Mr Perfect is nonexistent and I felt fine because it never reached a serious level. I mean, the sex was ok but looking back, he was probably pretending when he made those pig noises. It was as easy as that. Ask a miser to take you to a posh restaurant and he will flee, as if from the scene of a murder. I can safely say that I concluded any further communication with Daryl because he was too tight fisted, although I did ask him to use a finger.

I was not going to settle for a scrounger and I was prepared to be cautionary from now on to guarantee that I didn't involve myself with that type of idiot again. Money wasn't something that was majorly important to me but I had to draw the line when I was paying to keep a relationship. Thinking now, all I had to do was spend nothing on him, then he would have dumped me first, sometimes I can be so ignorant towards simplicity.

Chapter 6

Marcus

Marcus Daniels is the most credible reason why I struggle to find a partner worthy of my love. I'm looking for someone who is flawless – that way I'll never be pissed off. Marcus wasn't the perfect man and he certainly had his flaws. He was average looking but had a smile what could warm the chilliest room. He was only slightly taller than me and I was one who never pursued a man under six feet tall, but sometimes my criteria was challenged by certain, special men – usually those with stunning smiles. Besides, I'd never dated a man with curly hair before – hair that was blonde and tousled like a Greek warrior. Marcus was a manager of a car showroom and was one of the hardest working men I knew. Truth was I was in love with him before we paired up. If your heart decides your partner before you've realised their flaws then your heart is in serious trouble. These days I surround myself with titanium barriers and only when I'm one hundred percent sure I have found my suitor will I then allow the demolition ball to knock come and knock them down.

If there is one rule we should all try to live by in the game of love then it should be to never ever, get involved with a friend. Women feel safe to have a man to talk to, it's good to hear advice from the other side sometimes – but little do we know that these friends are usually acting as our best buddies because deep down they just want to get into our knickers. It's a truth that could be held viable in a courtroom. If you want male friends then make sure they are gay

– the heterosexual types are too complicated. More often than not, when a man and woman are friends, one is usually attracted to the other. We see that by having a male companion to lean on without the sexual or intimate tie is a blessing, however they always have a secret agenda, one that involves seeing us naked.

I had been friends with Marcus for about three years and nobody could make me laugh as much as he did. He had the weirdest sense of humour, yet so did I. We would sit for hours just taking the absolute piss out of everyone and we could make three hours feel like three minutes – we were that funny! I met Marcus through an old friend and always had a secret crush on him. He never seemed to be very popular with the ladies, although I couldn't see why. He had the cutest face and a magnificent personality to go with it. Sound perfect? I thought so! There was something really intriguing about him, he was highly addictive and I craved for his company. He fascinated me so much that I tried to Google him when he wasn't with me. I wanted to get to know him on a different level, being friends wasn't the only option for me. I knew that I would be taking a big risk by taking the friendship to the next level because if things didn't work out then I would be losing one of my favourite people. We had been flirting for years but never did anything due to the fact that we were both in relationships and the opportunity never arose. Whilst I had spent the past few months messing about with endless arseholes, the one I had always wanted had recently become available. I hadn't seen him for weeks and missed him like crazy, there were no doubts in my mind that he had always felt the same way about me. It was undisputable. Despite my nihilism, I was willing to bet on him and put my heart on the line. I was ready dive into the twisted game of love. Marcus was a man I deemed perfect for three years so surely I was right about him...surely!

I was out one night with two girlfriends. We had just devoured a delightful three course meal and all of us were slightly inebriated from the advantage of a free bar. I knew that Marcus had been out with his friends and we had been flirting copiously since we had both become single. I was confident that he felt the same way about me as I did him. Every time he used to leave my house, I would close the front door and whisper to myself 'I love you' because I was too gutless to say it to his face. Since we both became available I decided that the flirting and innuendos had to stop, it was time to take action. It was about two in the morning and I'd sent him a drunken text asking him if he 'fancied a chat'. I knew it was a ridiculous time to conduct a conversation but he knew what I was like when I'd had a drink, so I thought 'what the hell'. It was about two minutes after I had sent him the message that he replied and accepted my offer. Clearly, he was also partial to a middle-of-the-night beverage. I was convinced that he knew I wanted more than his conversation. He always unburdened his one night stands to me and the disastrous situations he got himself into. Truthfully, I knew he was a dead-cert and I wasn't just after a chat. We met and we went back to my house where more wine was consumed. I was drunk and tired, but hadn't felt so alive in a long time.

We talked for hours about anything and everything and after clearing three bottles of wine, we both anticipated taking our friendship to the next level. So many thoughts were running through my mind. Do I lean in to kiss him? Do I drop the remote control and promiscuously bend over to retrieve it? Instead, I asked him to assist me in taking off my dress. I'd always been forward before so why should I stop now. It worked a treat. From recollection, I would say if sex was an Olympic sport, there would have definitely been gold medals swinging from our sweaty necks.

I woke up late morning still on the couch and still in his arms. It was so surreal and I had to look at him over and over because everything felt like a dream. It was a strange feeling to be in a clinch with my best friend but, there wasn't any regret in my mind, only thoughts of a blossoming future. We were too perfect for each other, it had to work. I felt two faced because I was going against everything I'd thought about everlasting love. I'd spent years proving quite successfully, that men were the enemy, none were worth the aggravation and none carry enough crucial qualities to accommodate a triumphant relationship. I looked on as he started to wake up.

'Good morning gorgeous.' He said without regret, 'how are you feeling?'

'I feel brilliant actually,' I didn't want to quite confess my undying love quite yet. 'Thanks for last night.'

'My pleasure,' replied Marcus, 'I always knew that one day we would end up in this position.'

From that comment alone, I knew that he had always felt something for me. What I wanted to do was leap off the couch and scream 'I FUCKING LOVE YOU' but there would have been a whopping great hole in my front door as he retreated, without a goodbye. One thing my experiment had taught me since, is that men hate things to develop too quickly. Any early signs of commitment and they run like the children they are.

I wanted to secure that we both wanted to venture into a relationship.

'I just want you to know that I don't have any regrets about last night and I really want to see you again.' I don't think that was too hasty, I was pointing out that I wanted more than a one night fling and that a relationship was on the cards.

'Why don't you come round to mine tonight, that way we can talk properly without interruption?' He sounded keen. Talking? Whatever!

YES! YES! YES! I wanted to jump on him and kiss his face a thousand times but I had to get a grip. Oh my God! I hadn't been like this for years. Not one of my previous boyfriends from the wanker try-outs made me feel anything like this. I had to remain slightly subdued, if I jumped in too soon I could end up getting hurt or much worse, hurt him. I was positive about this relationship and immediately developed a belief that soul mates really do exist.

That evening, we were both quite inaudible. I think the fact that we were both tired and sober added to the awkward silence. At the time I didn't think much of it, I assumed that the reason for the silence was because we were both still in shock by what had happened the night before – plus we were alcohol free and exhausted. Despite the hushed atmosphere, I felt wonderful and we cuddled up in front of the television. I left after a couple of hours because I had to be up early for work. When I left, he sent a text to my phone, explaining how good he felt that we were together and left me with a flattering list of compliments. Why didn't he just say that in the room that time forgot? I didn't think much about it really, I was on such a high that he was finally mine besides; I took great pleasure in re-reading my complimentary text messages.

Over a three month period we shared some really memorable times. We would regularly sit together, curl up and watch movies. We went to concerts, restaurants, bars, and hung out with great friends. Life was great, he was gorgeous and he was mine. I wanted to keep him forever and I actually thought that I was transforming into a new woman. I would feel guilty about how much I used to snarl at the women who claimed to have the perfect partner. I was becoming one of those women and was beginning to believe that after three glorious months, it was possible to be happy and in love.

We had gone to a long anticipated rock gig in a nearby town. I had bought him the tickets as a surprise and I had been excited about it for the past month. I really made the effort to look good for him however, the fact that I'd tried on a trillion outfits made me slightly late. I rushed to his house because we had to catch the bus; I wanted the night to be special because after three months I thought it was long overdue to tell him how I really feel about him. We were always affectionate with each other but always avoided talking about our feelings. The reason I hadn't expressed my true thoughts were because of my knowledge of men in the past, if we say 'love' they think 'shove'. I thought that three months of what we had experienced was enough to convey my feelings. Not in a Shakespearian manner but enough for him to rip off my dress and reciprocate my love.

I arrived at his house slightly late. As he opened the door, I held the smile of a dental model; I was so energized about the evening. The look on his face was definitely not one which mirrored my expression.

'For fuck sake, you're half an hour late, I said be here at six.'

'Ok,' I thought. I was late but we still had time to catch the bus. I ignored his rude welcome. As I was in his house, I glared with bewilderment as he started to read a book, sat on the couch. Was I missing something here? We now had five minutes to leave and I was watching him fucking read. I didn't understand and he didn't look in the happiest of moods.

'We have to leave now babe, or we'll miss the bus.' I gulped. He glared at me with what seemed like disgust. It was like I'd asked him to clean my fridge.

'Not nice waiting, is it?' He vengefully replied.

I'd worked him out from that single comment. He was punishing me for being late and he wanted to make me uncomfortable for my behaviour. If I'd been a naughty girl, I wished it wasn't for being late. Deep down, I was irate because I was late through spending so much time agonising what to wear – to impress him! What I wanted to say was 'fuck you, grow up and get your whining arse out the door.'

Normally, I would respond with such a harsh statement, but the evening had been running through my thoughts for weeks. I told myself that he'd probably had a bad day at work and was using my lateness as an excuse to get rid of some testosterone. I kept my mouth tightly shut.

When we got to the bus stop, he bumped into an old friend and his attitude changed. He suddenly started to act happy again. He conversed like a champion. After standing at his side waiting for him to introduce me, I noticed that he hadn't spoken to me since he had re-acquainted himself with whatshisname. He even sat on a different seat to me on the bus why he continued discussing happy times with the elusive friend. For a while, I sat there in absolute shock. I felt like shouting over 'HELLO, IT'S ME, YOUR FUCKING GIRLFRIEND!' I was a friendless girl in a single seat with what seemed to hold the power of invisibility. I bet if I'd have stuck two fingers up to his friend I would get noticed then. I even considered taking my top off.

When we reached our destination, I was hoping that he had stopped sulking about my late arrival and was ready to rock the night away. We reached the venue and the only option for me was alcohol. I knew if I got a few beers down his neck he would be giddy Marcus again, the man I knew and loved.

It worked. After a few bottles of lager, he placed his arm around me and explained that he was just tired before and didn't mean to take it out on me. He kissed me and expressed his glorious smile, revealing his beautifully white teeth. All was forgiven. It was worrying how easy it was to forgive his behaviour. What else would I have forgiven him for? I swear, if any other bloke had treated me like that, I would have gone to the concert without him.

The actuality was that I was in love, and that was incredibly rare for me. I surprised myself that I actually kept my mouth closed.

The gig was amazing and we spent most of the night singing and dancing in each other's arms. I'd completely forgotten how he had made me look non-existent in front of his friend.

After a fantastic show, we headed home, picked up a pizza and went to his house. I felt so good that the past three months left me in a state of grace. I felt it was about time I told him how I felt. I was so nervous. I thought the famous three words would never leave my lips again but my lips were trembling that much I couldn't withhold it any longer.

'Marcus, I love you, you know.' There was a horrible silence; I swear I'd been stood there so long that mould was developing on the pizza. 'Speak, please speak,' I thought. Nothing, he just carried on eating his pizza. This was awkward. Had he heard me properly? I deliberated for a few minutes and came to the conclusion that he hadn't heard the words, which I struggled to get out. I tried again, 'I love you!'

'I heard you the first time, I just ignored you.' Once more he carried on eating. Once more I felt like I had done something seriously wrong. In one night I had arrived late and told my boyfriend of three months that I loved him. How inconsiderate of me, I didn't deserve to live! I must be the biggest bitch in the world to treat my boyfriend with such disrespect and indecency. I had to get to the bottom of it.

'Have I said something wrong?' He turned and looked at me with the same look he threw at me earlier.

'Why did you have to go and ruin the night by saying shit like that?' He was clearly not in the same place as I was.

'I'm sorry. I thought it was a good time to say it.'

Again, he turned to me. 'There is never a good time to say it.'

There it was – the flaw! I thought I had done it right this time. Even though he seemed the most perfect of men he turned out to be another Mr Wrong. My heart was pounding and I wanted to hurl on his pizza. I felt numb and was mystified by the whole conversation. I urged him to explain.

'I don't understand, the past three months have been amazing, I thought we felt the same about one another. Surely you knew how I felt about you? I thought you felt the same?' I shed an extremely rare tear.

He put his head in his hands and seriously looked stressed by the whole conversation, it was like he had been taken over by another being. The alien stood up and sighed,

'You have ruined everything now; we were fine till you came out with all that shit.' I'm not sure exactly what else he said because I got up and left the house where the thought of love shook the walls like a ten on the richter scale.

I cried all night, and those sad, lonely nights turned into weeks. I'd never felt so empty. Even though 'love' was prohibited I still yearned to be with him.

After a few lousy weeks, we finally talked. He explained how much he missed me and that he had issues with the L word. His excuse was that he loved a girl once before and she had broken his heart. Sure, I could get on board with that, I'd been hurt in the past and that's why I lived a pessimistic life and viewed men as losers and a complete waste of air. I tried to understand and we decided to give our relationship another try.

An incredible twelve months passed by. We laughed about everything, spent quality time together and things were looking promising. I told him regularly that I loved him but still never got a response back. I believed that he did love me in his own weird way, he just couldn't express it the same as I could. We had our little rows but that is like any couple. We always sorted out our differences because I was convinced that he was my soul mate, I always did.

I was always aware that Marcus had an eye for the girls, I trusted him and he would openly admit that he was sexually charged. He always swore that he would never cheat on me. I was fine with that and knew that most of the time when he commented about another girl it was to wind me up. He did things like that all the time, I always knew he liked to wind me up – that was one of the special, notwithstanding, weird things, which made our relationship solid.

I was seriously beginning to believe that Marcus was the one. I often pictured myself in a wedding dress and what it would be like to be juxtaposed with him at the ceremony. All our friends would be there; we would leave early and spend our honeymoon in bed. Both of us were level-headedly successful in our careers and I thought if we lived together and got hitched, the world would belong to us. Had my search ended? Was I now a member of the elite? One of the happy women in the world? I wanted to apologize to every woman I snarled at over the years. Life was good.

I was aware that Marcus was a little obnoxious and set in his ways – as well as being negated from expressing sincere sentiment but I knew it was in him somewhere, hidden under his tough exterior. I was learning that keeping a healthy relationship wasn't simple; it had to be worked on relentlessly. That was the first time that I was optimistic about a relationship, even though I was dismissing my practiced morals and principles. I was a hypocrite to myself. Had I grown up or met my match?

If I had to say something about his misdemeanours, it would be the notion that he could never see things my way. If I was upset, he never understood why. He was a relationship virgin and I was breaking him in. If he ever offended me and he often did, he couldn't quite snatch why I had steam coming out of every outlet. The focal reason why we argued was because he failed to understand why I was pissed off with him.

The final argument we had will be imbedded in my memory forever. He had just returned from his weekend with the boys. We were sat on my couch one night and I was drinking the wine, which he'd brought back for me.

Marcus and I had just eaten a lovely meal together and as usual, he was thankful for my hospitality. One of my favourite things about him was that he was continually well-mannered. That fateful night I snuggled up to him on the couch, no television, just the sound of our voices. I'd missed him terribly. We were joking with one another until the subject of his holiday came up. He liked to tell me about his cheeky antics and how much fun he would have laughing with his friends because he knew I would generally joke and laugh with him. The fact that we enjoyed one another's company and laughed together was the main reason that we hooked up in the first place. Marcus took it upon himself to raise a conversation which was introduced as 'funny'. I anticipated the quips.

'It was so funny on the last day of the holiday,' giggled Marcus. 'Three other lads and I were leaving the hotel and these girls were topless outside. They let us have our photo taken with them. Can you believe that one of them had fake tits... she let us squeeze them. Fucking brilliant.'

I really don't know how I held back an eruption of hysterics; what was wrong with me? Had I finally lost my sense of humour? He seemed to be amused with the prelude so I asked him to continue...

'Go on.'

'Well, they were on their way to their rooms just as we were leaving for the airport and they were all really drunk.' He was actually enjoying telling the story. 'They invited us in their room but obviously we said no because we had to catch the plane.' He noticed my changing expression. My sarcastic, pretending-to-be-interested grin had turned into a snarl. 'What's up with your face?' He asked. 'I swear to you nothing happened; it was just funny.'

I took a deep breath. 'We had to catch the plane? Nothing

happened? BOLLOCKS! What type of a fucking teacup do you take me for?' I was not pleased in the slightest.

'I had a feeling you would react like this.' He was somewhat ignorant again towards my feelings. 'I thought you, more than anyone would see the funny side.' I couldn't believe what I was hearing. 'You know I would never cheat on you, it was funny that's all.' There was that word again, 'funny'. Any normal functioning bloke would never take it upon himself to tell his girlfriend that he had partaken in such a seedy, adolescent act. I failed to share his joy. I composed myself and went into the kitchen for a cigarette. I don't know what angered me the most, the fact that he happily grabbed the fake tits, the fact that the plane stopped him from going to their room or the fact that he actually thought I would laugh about it. How should I have reacted? Applaud him, say 'well done you!' Was he for fucking real?

I composed myself again and rushed back to the living room to see if the comedian was still on stage. Thank God, he was still there, I almost missed the rest of the show.

'I think you're just being soft,' he said.

I think he was genuinely offended because I didn't share his joy. How selfish of me again, I really needed to lighten up. Any normal loving girlfriend would have been in raptures of laughter, I'm sure.

That night was the last I ever spent with Marcus. I couldn't believe that after twelve months he still hadn't grasped the real concept of a relationship. Every time we argued it was always I who instigated a reunion and made the first move. This time I left things as they were and I never heard from him again. No contact was further proof that I inflated his ego. He thrived off the fact that I loved him but I would never receive the same dedication. I had been a mug and he had drunk me dry. Years of friendship was obliterated because he had issues. I was devastated for months but I learned from my experience and realised that he was just another man. He was someone who was adored by everyone and someone who made an incredible friend. He was an amazing guy, but he had a serious flaw, which he would never overcome – not for me anyway. I'm just glad I realised it sooner rather than later. Maybe one day we'll speak again. Our friendship was flawless, we just weren't matched emotionally, and I wasn't the one.

I stand by my earlier testimony that the perfect man does not exist. We can fall in love and get married but complete fulfilment is unattainable. Some women can overcome such flaws, but not me. I don't want a miser, geek, egotistical idiot or a robot who can't express his feelings. From now on I will stick with my friends because they are the ones who stand by me through the good and bad times. I still lived in hope of love and longevity but Mr Right was being maintained a falsified terminology.

Chapter 7

The Ego

One thing I learned from finding a flaw early on was that it was much easier to move forward. By not committing to anyone kept me guarded – there was an unstoppable force field surrounding my heart and only very few broke through it. My barriers were up and I would only force them down once I knew that the relationship was one worthy enough to work on. Furthermore, there wasn't much stress by using my defences, this I favoured. A lot of the time, I was content with work, life and using my spare time to focus on myself. For any single woman, time alone is necessary – to recharge the batteries, so to speak. It was so easy to revert to my everyday routine without any baggage, but I was subconsciously on the lookout for a new ex boyfriend. There was no urgency, I knew it wouldn't be long before I was sat facing another imbecile. Sometimes I mused during alone time, about my fate in the quest for love. Despite my cynicism, I knew there had to be somebody with whom I could relate. There had to be!

There was one peculiarity, which struck me. Once I consciously decided to get back in the game and put myself out there, I struggled to receive any attention, never mind hooking up with someone. Once I decided that I have had enough and mentally conclude myself from any male communication I seem to attract them like blood initiating a shark's feeding frenzy. The majority of men I have known or heard about are players themselves. They are aware of the no strings situation and I have realised that when you are desperate for love you are simply just a target for easy sex. If men sensed I didn't want anything serious then it's easier to seal a date. Trust me, tell a man you are not looking for anything serious and you will be bombarded with calls, texts and dates, until you've had sex of course, then it's over. I often wonder if I am going to build myself a reputation as a whore or maniser but I truly believe in equal opportunities. If they can do it then so can I!

After weeks of booze, parties and reacquainting myself with friends, I decided that I needed a new look to coincide with my newer self; the woman who had taken a break from dating. I decided to visit a hair salon after realising I wasn't setting much of a trend with the grey streaks, which I'd had in for a while, so I was more determined to impress. Admittedly, I'm not a fan of the salon and the ridiculously priced treatments but if I was going to reinvent myself then I had to keep up with the image obsessed society which I occupied.

Whilst discussing holidays, weather, work and conducting conversations with complete strangers, I was contemplating suicide with the scissors. The stylist insisted on knowing the biography of my life as I sat in boredom whilst I tried to avoid looking like I was in love with myself due to the huge mirror I was forced to sit in front of. Instead of admiring myself for two hours, I looked beyond my reflection to nosey around the salon. To the left of the mirror was a young man having streaks. It was difficult to tell the colour because his hair was stuck up with foil but it was an amusing sight and passed a bit of time, until I was busted. I was so busy trying to escape staring at myself that I didn't realise he'd noticed me grinning at his metallic strands. The moment he'd clocked me felt like a lifetime and was interrupted when he spoke,

'Is there a reason why you find my appearance so funny?'

SHIT! I had to think quickly, if I didn't reply I would look like a total stuck up bitch...

'No, not at all,' I responded the best I could, 'I was just thinking about the roast chicken I have to cook later.' There was an uncomfortable pause for a moment and eventually he laughed at my ridiculous comment.

'Oh, I get it; you're referring to the foil, yeah, very funny.'

I thought I'd better not elaborate on his hilarious appearance as I'd broken the ice and cut the tension. It was a good time to develop the conversation.

'I'm Roxy. Sorry, I didn't mean to make you uncomfortable. I'm not a regular and I'm not used to the salon environment, the glare from your foils caught my eye.' Oh dear, I was flirting again, I was becoming an expert. Any chance to instigate a relationship I was on it – I was becoming a man! I tried to inform myself that I was in the salon to reinvent myself. I was supposed to be taking a break from any interaction or association with the opposite sex.

'No worries,' he replied, 'I come here every six weeks to get my roots done. I'm Cody, by the way.'

He was Cody Richards, a man with a tan and a smile that could induce ovulation. I tried to stop myself from laughing aloud by the thought that he actually got his roots done every six weeks. I wasn't used to seeing men obsess over their looks. One ex boyfriend only showered once a week and thought that was acceptable. I still have a pair of his boxer shorts in my drawer – I only pray that he bought some more because it was the only pair he had. Personal hygiene is essential; nobody wants to curl up with an unshaven, sweaty man with a week's worth of toe-jam stinking out the house! To bathe, deodorize and regularly clean the teeth is enough to keep a woman happy, however, when it is taken to the extreme, women can become jealous.

I looked through the mirror and briefly considered that Cody might be gay – heterosexual men couldn't look so good surely? Once my hair was blow dried to perfection I deliberately flicked my hair in his direction and noticed he was highlighted blonde. I admit he looked pretty damn good. The blonde streaks complimented his tanned appearance and accentuated the whiteness of his teeth. His teeth were as white as the wedding dress that morphed in my mind. The fact that we departed the salon at the same time created a perfect time to talk more – somewhere that didn't stink of peroxide and anywhere where we could enjoy the normality of facing one another instead of mirror flirting.

I asked him out for a drink without hesitation and he didn't dither to accept either. It was always a massive confidence boost when a good looking man wants to be seen in public with you. However, I remember Reece Evans. He preferred to boost several women's confidence at the same time, the women just didn't know it.

I had never been on a date with a blonde haired person before and I even considered that dark haired men possibly carried the worst behaviours, as if they possessed a faulty gene or something. I'd only really been attracted to brunettes. I was praying that his sexuality was as straight as his teeth and I kept thinking that if I could pull someone who embodied the appearance of a catalogue model then there's a chance he could be gay. I'm sure he wasn't because he spoke to my chest and that's a secure sign of heterosexuality. I'm not one to judge a book by its cover but when you come across one so glossy and without creases then I had to give him the benefit of the doubt. He looked so good that I overlooked my choice to take respite from men and I succumbed to my feminine needs. What was wrong with me? Did I have low self esteem and becoming one of those women who couldn't be alone? A multitude of self doubting thoughts overpowered my mind, I actually felt sick. I'd been so occupied that no man was right for me that every man I met instigated instantaneous negativity. Maybe he was one of the good guys. I couldn't judge him because he liked to look after himself. I'm not usually a woman with poor self regard but I was slightly bemused as to why he seemed as keen as I was. I knew that there are certain leagues in the dating game. I considered myself average looking so I should approach average looking men. This situation was breaking the boundaries, I was division three and he was premiership. I know looks aren't everything but they do help!

I mused as to why Cody was single (if he was single) and I was eager to find his essential flaw. The next day I took a taxi to his local pub to meet for a few drinks and to see how we related with one other. When I arrived he was surrounded by girls. I didn't feel threatened at first, but a little nervous when he made a beeline for me and the girls stared, each one held a look of constipation on their faces.

He actually looked pleased to see me, 'I'm so glad you came.' Ok, so far so good!

I mumbled like a jittery teen. 'I've been looking forward to it. I see you have a fan club.' He turned to look at the four girls behind us.

'Oh, don't worry about them, two are my ex girlfriends and the other two just want to get into my pants.' He held a straight face.

GREAT! He'd invited me to a pub where I was now public enemy number one. I commented on the uncomfortable situation I was forced to be in. 'I don't mean to be petty or paranoid but the staring and pointing is a big giveaway.'

He laughed at the situation, 'Don't worry about them, they always glare when I meet someone new.' I suddenly felt sorry for the women who were clinging onto hope that they may get a chance to be with him again. With him, parading other girls in front of them was for his own ego and to be honest, it was undeniably cruel. 'Lucky me,' I thought. I should be so honoured I'd been chosen. I had become an accessory in his game and I could tell he loved it. I wanted to leave but I had to give him the benefit of the doubt. I was still out to prove that Mr Right did not exist and the odds were certainly in my favour so far.

Despite the deathly glances and whisperings of slag, bitch and fucking tramp I loosened up and we had an unexpectedly, average date. We discussed likes and dislikes and I discovered that he liked himself very much and disliked anyone who didn't like him. Fair enough, he was honest but carried off his manner with blatant arrogance. I was still trying not to judge, he was just a little sure of himself and I was inclined to see him again in a less psychotic environment. He walked me to the car park where I waited for my taxi home. It felt better to breathe at a normal pace again without the killer quartet breathing down my neck even though I was sure I could hear their teeth grinding from inside. I told him we had to meet somewhere less life threatening next time because I feared for my life. I would have been more relaxed if I had shit my pants during the date rather than worry about having my eyes clawed out.

As my taxi pulled into the car park, he leaned towards me and kissed me on my forehead. 'I'll meet you on Saturday at the park, I like it there.' I was impressed and glad he wanted to meet in a mutual place. It sounded quite romantic and I maybe he portrayed himself differently in a peaceful, non alcoholic environment. He turned and stuck his fingers up at the four faces pressed up against the window.

'I'm sorry about them, I'll have a word. I can't help it if they find me irresistible, can I?' Oh my God! I rushed to the taxi in case he kissed me again; I couldn't let that happen when his head had just been up his arse. I waved and gestured to let him know I would ring him about Saturday.

I spent a couple of days reflecting on my time with Cody and whether there was any point in going through with our second date.

Saturday arrived and I promised myself that I would try and waiver his self-importance and enjoy a relaxing atmosphere in the park. I already had a mind overflowing with doubts and I talked myself into going. Was I obsessed with dating or was I obsessed with finding that damn flaw? My single life had become a social experiment. I was confusing myself with what I actually wanted from life. I did want to settle down but I was convinced that I was cursed to meet types that I had been accustomed to. The type I would call Dick Head! Cody was fifteen minutes late for the park, I wasn't surprised or angry for that matter, which was strange. Usually, I'm so hot headed that I would have been scuffing the end of my shoe, kicking a tree. Why wasn't I bothered if he arrived or not?

Cody did arrive eventually and to be honest, I was calm and quite proud of myself for remaining that way. Was this a sign of age? He walked over casually, holding his jacket over his shoulder like a poser from the Great Universal catalogue, accepting the glances and smiles from lady dog walkers.

'Hi, sorry I'm late,' said Cody. He stank of expensive aftershave.

We situated ourselves on a bench under a willow tree and in front of the lake. He leaned back with both hands behind his head and inhaled the summer's day, 'Ah, I love coming here when I get any spare time.' He didn't strike me as someone who was close to nature.

'What else do you do in your spare time?' I questioned.

'I go to the gym of course!' He spoke as if I'd insulted his physical appearance somewhat. Before I had a chance to comment, he continued... 'Followed by a sun bed session, sauna and a shower. Normally after I would come here and unwind and maybe hit the town in the evening.'

'So you don't work then?' I was suddenly disheartened and realized that I was sitting next to a work shy egotist.

'I don't have time to work, I'd have to get up during the night to work out and stuff. It doesn't bear thinking about, I would look a mess.'

There it was the flaw I so eagerly anticipated. He only had time for himself and himself only. Here was I feeling flattered because he'd brought me to his special place but I learned that the only reason he loved it so much was because the lake we sat in front of was a giant substitute mirror. By sitting on the bench he could observe himself endlessly as the rippled water reflected his rippled muscles. What an arse! I deliberated for a moment just how I was going to deal with such a conceited prick. I concluded that looks really aren't the be all and end all of relationships and sure he looked awesome but I would always feel inferior to Mr Magnificent so I decided to do what I do best and that was to take the piss out of him. I looked at him whilst he lay back on the bench and flexed his pectorals.

'I'll have to go any minute; I need to clip my toenails.' His face edged away from his chest as his frown displayed confusion.

'You said we could spend the afternoon together, now suddenly you have to go?' I don't think he was used to someone of the opposite sex expressing a need to leave so hastily.

'If I don't cut them, they start to dig in my shoes and I can't risk that,' He was so self-indulged that he didn't even notice my sarcasm.

'Stay here with me, you will forget about the nails.' He was actually being serious. 'Hey, look, I've restyled my hair. Thought I'd go for a side parting, what do you think? I've had loads of attention since I tried it.' I couldn't stomach anymore supercilious shit.

'Actually I prefer brunettes myself, the blonde looks okay but I think it suits the younger lads.' Suddenly his smarmy grin changed to a picture of horror.

'What the hell are you on about, I'm only twenty five!' He was far from impressed.

'Twenty five? Really? Honestly I thought you were at least thirty.'

It was difficult not to smirk at his dismay. 'I don't mean to be rude but you've surprised me.' If he had been eating at that moment I would be performing the Heimlich manoeuvre right there and then.

'You cheeky cow! Have you any idea how many girls would kill for the chance to be here with me right now?' The nastiness kicked in, I obviously hit him where it hurt, how dare I insult such a marvellous creation and I had only just started.

'All I'm saying is that I've been out with better looking men, don't be offended, you do look good, but you're not my type that's all.' I decided to leave, I hadn't brought any tissues and I think he was going to cry.

'I'm everybody's type!' Cody was beyond insulted.

'You're not mine.' I left the bench feeling satisfied that I'd knocked his self-worth even for a short moment. I don't think it's acceptable to knock someone's appearance because I had been a victim of this in the past but there is only so much egotism I can take. I was sure that he would bounce back as soon as he saw his reflection again. I was not going to become one of his cling ons and actually felt sorry for the potty parasites in the pub. A man who looks so good is never a safe bet for a solid relationship anyway, they always receive attention from other girls that would be ready to pounce on him when your back is turned. If that man is aware he looks that good then I stay well clear, he would never love anyone but himself and if you cannot tell that man what he wants to hear then you are history. Stick with the average guy, that was my new plan. I mean, of course I feel honoured and privileged to be in the presence of such superiority but it was time to move on.

Chapter 8

The Toyboy

It had been a few of months since I last dated anyone. This is something that displeased me greatly. A break was refreshing but I wasn't getting any younger and my sentimental side tapped me on the shoulder from time to time and reminded me that I was just a girl at heart who wanted to be loved. I came to the conclusion that I had used up my cretin cards including the joker so maybe, just maybe, an ace was due to come my way. The break had given me time to reflect on previous misdemeanours and I was damn sure that I was wise enough to spot the traditional idiot; I'd had enough, that's for sure! My friends always told me that you meet people when you least expect it – stop looking and let serendipity happen.

I looked outside the window and the sun was stretched like a beautiful canvas. I looked in the mirror beside the fireplace and pathetically scrutinised that I wasn't a fresh canvas anymore, I was becoming antique. I was feeling my age creeping up drastically and I was getting quite acclimatised to Saturday nights with a DVD and a bottle of supermarket branded wine. There was nothing wrong with choosing a bath and film over a night on the town was there? It wasn't just my actions that were portraying my late thirties, it was my appearance too. Every morning I looked in the mirror and saw the lines appearing before my tired, weary eyes. The lines that portrayed my overuse of frowning were becoming permanently indented and when looking down, I could only see lumps of flesh where my nipples used to be. Collagen creams were another useless marketing ploy that raised hopes of youth and eternal beauty and without surgery, other women my age and I were suffering through our reflections. In my brooding horror, I felt that the only way financially was to caulk my face – the situation was getting that intense.

Did I really need consecutive dates to feel attractive? Maybe my shallowness was now becoming my karma. My criteria were endless. My prospective partner needed to have a full head of hair with no signs of receding. The body of Adonis was not entirely necessary but he must possess a relatively structured body so my hands could move freely without blockages. He would have to be of high intelligence, which included a spectacular sense of humour and incredible charm. He would have to dress appropriately for the desired occasion and remain completely ardent regarding our relationship. Marcus was the only one who had fit the bill, despite his own unacceptable traits – my recent dating record proved this.

There comes a point in a woman's life where she must make a stand and accept the ageing process, embrace it and make important decisions to where she should be and what she expects from life. Time moves progressively fast and I was painfully aware that I had reached the stage that every woman reaches before the age of forty – midlife crisis!

My premenopausal worries were so intense that I had to ring my optimistic friend Helen to hear some words of virtue and hope before I put on my slippers and conformed to mutton hood and ridicule. The thought of growing old alone began to terrify me so much that premonitions of twenty cats purring around my feet were scarily realistic to the point of hallucination. Tears crashed from my heavily lined eyes as I shakily dialled the number – alas, she was home.

'Hi Helen, it's me.' My voice was whiny.

'Roxy, is that you?' Answered Helen. I was despondent with my reply

'Yes... I'm having a crisis and I just need a little optimism right now.'

'Ok, ok, just calm down,' replied Helen softly and calmly. 'What's happened?'

'I've turned into my mother overnight.' I was serious!

'Your mother?' Said Helen. 'What are you talking about?'

My sarcastic and scornful explanations were the only way Helen understood my current predicament, she knew me better than anybody. 'It's gone Helen, it's gone.'

'What's gone?' Helen asked.

'My youth! I've had it, I'm overcooked.' The tears were replaced with a splenetic tone.

'Don't talk stupid, Roxy,' said Helen, 'you look fantastic for your age.'

'You have to say that because you're my best friend,' I assumed. 'I'm looking in the mirror right now and I see a gigantic raisin in front of me. Have you noticed I haven't had any interest from men in months? I may as well join the darts and dominoes team because that's the only way I'm ever going to get laid again.' The mere thought of hitting on the beer bellied gents reinforced my terror of becoming a more senior citizen.

'You're being ridiculous, Roxy,' lectured Helen. 'Listen honey...' I interrupted.

'Call me dear.' I replied.

Helen sighed heavily down the phone. 'You are just having a bad day. I feel like that sometimes. You need to stop thinking like this. So what? You haven't had any interest in a while, it does happen, plus you haven't been going out as much. Besides, you always look amazing when you go out. Maybe you need to get dressed up this weekend and have some fun? You need a bit of flattery that's all; we all do, especially at our age. You look younger than most women in their thirties.'

'Helen?' I replied. 'I have wrinkles on my forehead.'

'So, we all get them and so do the men you date.' Helen was trying to rationalise the situation. 'You look fabulous and you know it, you're just having a senior moment.'

'My head looks like a barcode.' I wasn't convinced of Helen's flattery.

'Shut up, you're being ridiculous.' Helen was becoming irate due to my lunacy. 'Right! We are going out this Saturday and I'm going to prove to you that you haven't lost your touch and you definitely don't look old. I'll explain to Scott and we are going to revive you. Let's go to that 80's bar, mingle with the other thirty something's and get you back on track. Ok?'

I wasn't overly enthusiastic, 'If we must... maybe I'll be offered the concessionary entry price.'

'Roxy!' Shouted Helen, 'have a nice, long bath and sort your head out. You are the most independent, confident woman I know. Stop this moping and I'll pick you up at seven on Saturday. I have to go to work now, are you going to be ok?'

'Yes,' I replied hastily. 'I'll see you on Saturday.'

I put down the phone and took one last look at my mother in the mirror. 'Get a grip Roxy.' Great! Not only did I look like a soon-to-be pensioner, I was talking to myself. Was dementia to become an added worry? As a usual positive person, I had absorbed some of Helen's coaxing and took myself upstairs to fill in the creases and head off to work. After all, she could be right. I hadn't been on a night out for at least a month so I'd not had any male attention. I had been dating incessantly for over twelve months – I think I was giving up on finding a suitable partner, I hadn't even come close. I could give in to spinsterhood and let the wankers win or I could get back on my bike and peddle harder. I needed a confidence boost and fast, just a quick fix to put me back on track and continue my pursuit!

Saturday soon came and Helen was late as expected. I opened the door wrapped in a towel, much to Helen's horror. I always took longer to get ready when I was going out with Helen because in the twenty years I'd known her, she had never successfully managed to arrive on time. I always thought about my wedding day and how I would need to inform her that the wedding was two hours before it actually was, just so she could be by my side. Typically, she was late but not as late as I'd anticipated, which made me look like a hypocrite.

'Aren't you ready?' She yelled.

'Calm down, Helen,' I replied, 'it'll take me half an hour tops. I only have to straighten my hair and get changed. Have a glass of wine and relax.'

'I can't relax – I haven't been out for months.' Helen was very excitable. Rightly so, she hadn't been going out as much since Scott expressed his disappointment that they never spent enough time together. It was good to see her settling down but I did miss my pulling partner. Scott is a good guy though, albeit it a tad boring. He looks after her and is a natural with the hoover, which was a prerequisite before Helen involved herself with anyone. More so, I don't ever remembering her being so happy. Their relationship was inspiring for me and hindered my fixation that all men were worthless. Every time I saw them together I was reminded what I once shared with Marcus, before he turned to the dark side. I wanted that again. I had learned about the rarity of happiness and I didn't blame her for holding onto it, despite losing my previously slutty sidekick.

I was ready and raring to go. I needed to prove that I could still be a competitor in Single Ville and I wasn't quite ready for the scrap heap just yet. Admittedly, I was excited about our evening ahead –

I hadn't been out for a month and I'm glad of that. Before, a night out seemed like a chore – it was routine. Being best friends with my couch for the past few weeks was a blessing in disguise, I just knew that I had to break that cycle of sitting on it and binge eating or I was going to start looking like a couch, then nobody would want to sit on me then.

Helen and I arrived at Duran, the best eighties bar in town. We hadn't been there in so long, I was keen to drop my handbag in the centre of the dance floor, drink cheekily titled cocktails and mouth the words to Wham! Helen loved eighties music, it reminded her when she was single and it was amusing to watch – till she'd consumed too many screaming orgasms. One drink too many and Helen transformed into a cock hungry mentalist. She would never cheat on Scott but receiving attention from men was a delight for her and embarrassing for me.

I returned from the bar and walked back to our table. Helen was on the dance floor again being ogled by the fortysomething's. She loved the attention – I could tell the way she rubbed her own behind whilst gyrating to Blondie. I sucked on the cocktail straw and waved to Helen discreetly as she tried to beckon me over. I was just about to walk over and rescue her from the lecherous line of men surrounding the dance floor's edge and I was tapped on the shoulder.

'Hello, can I buy you a drink?' A handsome, young man stood before me. Truth is I had to look over my own shoulder to check if there was a twenty year old girl behind me. Was he talking to me?

'Me?' I replied.

'Yes, of course you,' he was adamant. From my first observation I guessed his age at twenty five. A tall lad with mousy coloured hair and a rugby player's body. Someone who I would love to make breakfast for ten years ago!

I smiled at him, still unsure as to why someone so young would be in an eighties bar. 'I'm Roxy.'

'Nice name. I'm Daniel but you can call me Danny.' His glance was one that I recognised when a man wanted to rip off my dress – I'm sure I wasn't misreading the signs.

'How old are you?' I had to ask.

'Twenty four.' He replied. I wasn't far off when I guessed at twenty five but I was feeling awkward knowing he was fourteen years my junior.

'How old are you?' Fuck, I was dreading that question. I should have kept my mouth shut. Do I lie about my age and ensue a night of passion to boost my own confidence or do I tell him the truth and walk home alone to be welcomed back by my couch and slippers? It was a tough decision.

'I'm thirty two.' I was a terrible liar.

'Wow, you look great for thirty two.' He genuinely appeared surprised. Not as surprised as me though. I was plainly bullshitting but was he? 'Are you here alone?' Asked Danny.

'No, of course not – I wouldn't turn out alone.' I laughed falsely. 'No, I'm with my friend Helen, she's just...' I looked onto the dance floor and Helen was grabbing her own crotch to a Michael Jackson song. I was cringing. 'Actually, I'm not sure where she is. She must have gone to the loo.'

Daniel and I conversed like lovesick puppies and for those few minutes, I felt alive. I was participating under a blatant lie but the visions of turning into my mother were erased, at least for one night. We swapped numbers and I wasn't confident that I would hear from him again but to be approached by a young, fit man was just the tonic I needed.

Daniel left with the promise that he would call the day after. Helen had missed the whole thing. I don't even think she was aware that I was still in the bar, never mind being chatted up by someone so young. He made me feel young and alive so I had no choice but to join Helen on the dance floor and take the edge off her humiliating herself. I was always a team player.

The following morning I woke up alone and looked in the mirror. I felt that instant regret when you realise you were too pissed to remove the make up from the night before. My eyes were heavy and blackened by the layers of mascara I'd applied the night before. Thank fuck Daniel didn't stay over because he would have seen the dramatic effect of my actual age. My face resembled Rocky Balboa's after the twelfth round.

I sat at my dressing table with my expensive cleanser, toner and moisturiser and took extra care around the eye area to ensure the mascara was gently removed from my many creases. Upon completion I was left facing a thirty eight year old single woman who truly appreciated the quality and effectiveness of good make up. I had to put some foundation on quickly before I was back on the phone to Helen, crying over my invading thoughts of becoming crazy, cat lady.

My phone started to ring. I looked down pleasantly surprised as the name 'Danny' was highlighted. My stomach turned as I answered.

'Hi Danny.' I was revived from my thoughts as Danny expressed his eagerness to take me out on a date. During our conversation I was distracted from the thoughts of cats and wrinkles. Maybe this is what I needed? A young man to keep me feeling young. Mentally anyway, I could easily fabricate a holiday to pursue some plastic surgery. He would never know!

Later that day, I met up with Danny at the bowling alley. Nobody had ever taken me bowling before. Even though this was probably a typical date for a twenty four year old, Danny showed more maturity than all previous mishaps. He was part of a different generation and very respectful to me. Every time I picked up the bowling ball, I would slyly turn my head so I could absorb the complimentary look on his face as he checked out my arse. I actually think he allowed me to win the game too, which was kind because I'm naturally competitive and had I lost he could have witnessed something quite psychotic. Danny wasn't embarrassed about being seen with me, despite random glances from people probably wondering if he was just really close to his mother. He held my hand all the way home and as he picked me up like a rugby ball and threw me onto my bed, I learned one crucial difference from men in their twenties and thirties – stamina!

I was officially a cougar and I had met my tiger. I'm sure at thirty eight I was a cougar but Danny believed I was thirty two, this was a lie that was haunting me every day we were together. He did often refer to me as a MILF, however I had no children so I didn't think that was a title I was worthy of. If I had children and Danny knew my real age and saw my morning appearance I'm sure that MILF would stand for Mum is looking Fucked!

Four weeks had passed and I was still holding up the barriers. I really liked Danny but I couldn't tell him the truth about my age. That was my flaw, if he knew it; I was a liar! I wouldn't have lied had I known he wanted a proper relationship but even if he did, I would never feel safe with someone so young. As soon as real thirty two year old showed interest, he'd be off and I'd be left old and alone with my cats and couch.

The day Danny and I broke up was when I realised the real truth behind his eagerness to be with an older woman. I initially thought it was because of my sexual prowess and experience in the bedroom. Another delusion of grandeur.

Danny came round to my flat with a beautiful bouquet of flowers. This particular day he was overly clingy – something that I wasn't fond of. It was nice to be held and spoiled but he could be so smothering that I had an inhaler on regular prescription. I put the flowers in the kitchen sink till I could be bothered to put them in a vase and Danny sat down on my couch.

'Roxy, sit down. I need to talk to you about something.' He sounded too serious for my liking. I obliged him and sat down on my friend, the couch.

'What's up?' I hastily replied. Danny took my hand and held it firmly. He gazed hopefully into my eyes.

'Listen, I've been discussing this with my Mum and she agrees with me. We've been getting serious over the past few weeks and I think I'm in love with you.' Oh shit! I was dreading this happening. The fact was I wasn't in love with him, I was enjoying the moments together and I loved how young he made me feel. He continued. 'How would you feel about me moving in here?' Double shit! That wasn't what I wanted. I had to tread carefully.

'Listen, Danny, I really like you. You're funny, kind, considerate and bloody good in the bedroom...' I paused to absorb his devastation.

'You don't want to, do you?' He replied with a sad tone. I felt terrible. I had used him to satisfy my own egotistical needs. I was so desperate for someone to reverse the ageing process that I didn't stop to think about what he wanted. It was too soon though whatever his age.

'I just don't see this going anywhere, Danny,' I responded in a calm tone. 'You are great but I'm too old for you. It's been a laugh and I've enjoyed your company but it won't work out long term. I'm sorry.'

Danny was more despairing, 'Ok, I'll prove it to you. Let's get married.' I had dug myself a massive hole and would have to endure dirty fingernails to climb back out of it.

'I can't marry you, Danny, I'm sorry. I'm just not in the same place as you.' I felt like a total bitch. 'I think we should end this now. It's too soon for me. I never expected things to go this far.'

'We can make it work. My friend lives with a woman who is ten years older, they are fine together.' He was becoming more agitated. I had no choice but to tell him the truth, I owed him that at least.

'I'm thirty eight, Danny. Thirty nine in a few weeks.' I said it like I was actually glad of my age.

'What!?' Replied Danny surprised. 'You said you were thirty two? You're almost old enough to be my mother.'

Funny how six years can change a person's perception of you. Danny stood up and grabbed his jacket. 'I can't believe I fell for that. I thought you looked older but I was just being nice.' His immaturity began to arise. 'You're well old.'

Danny left, slamming the front door behind him. I was relieved that the relationship was over because there's no point being with somebody if there is no future, no matter how much stamina they have. I learned a valuable lesson never to lie about my age again even though for just a few short weeks, I felt young and wanted. When Danny left I was left looking back at my ageing reflection. My marital clock was ticking and I had no time to waste. I was still adamant that I wasn't going to settle for anyone, I was consumed with finding a perfect suitor – someone who understood me and someone who I could wake up to without a giving a single fuck about my panda eyes.

Chapter 9

The Gaming Addict

There comes a time in every woman's life when she drops the barriers for someone who surpasses her expectations. Someone so fanciable that the mere thought of them naked warranted afternoon masturbation. When you meet someone initially and those butterflies tickle your stomach like at the top of a rollercoaster ride then sometimes you have to take the plunge and go for it because something spectacular may just happen.

It wasn't until I met Aaron Jones that I truly let my guard down for the first time since Marcus. It wasn't planned but all I can say is that the heart wants what the heart wants, and mine was beating loudly for Aaron. You could call it a whirlwind romance. It was at first. The relationship was full of passion, communication, honesty and no-holds-barred sex. He looked at me with piercing eyes and consistently repeated how much he wanted to be with me and this was my vision of the perfect man. The one I had waited for so longingly. He was two years younger than me, although admittedly he looked his age, but he possessed the looks of a Hollywood movie star.

I was introduced to Aaron at a friend's party. He'd recently broken up with a girl and was at the stage where he was seeking someone to get under to get over her. When he entered the room, I was in the right frame of mind to oblige – he was more enticing than that last bit of wine in the bottle. You know you're smashed out of your head but you can't leave it in there as you inform yourself that it might go off? As soon as I laid eyes on Aaron, I strutted past him, giving him my flirty face. He reciprocated by looking me up and down – a trait common amongst most players. Was he a player? This is how we made acquaintance with one another...

I stood with Linda, propping up the kitchen unit, half-baked. 'Is that Aaron guy still coming who you told me about?'

'I thought you weren't bothered about Aaron? Actually, your words were 'I couldn't give a toss?' Linda was smirking because she knew me more than most. She knew that if the Hunchback of Notre dame wanted to take me out I would still welcome the attention- any single lady would, right? I lit up a cigarette.

'I'm not bothered but I was interested in what type of guy you thought I preferred, or if this was some joke and a ninety year old was going to walk through the door. I'm only here out of morbid curiosity.' Linda expressed a disappointed look. 'Oh, and I'm here to see you of course. I love your parties. The food is awesome, your friends are cool.' I think I redeemed myself.

Linda reciprocated my comment with a giant hug. She was always very affectionate when she'd had a drink and loved nothing more but to laugh – that's something I loved about her.

I stood in the kitchen as Linda walked to the front door. I was assuming a casual position against the kitchen worktop, pretending to listen to some of Linda's older friends. I kept my head sideways so I didn't look eager to see him – that would have been a disaster. There's no bigger turn off for a man if the woman presents herself as desperate, I know this from many experiences of acting desperate. I remember telling one guy that I loved him on the third date. It sounds ridiculous but he was gorgeous, rich and well-endowed; who wouldn't try to bag him early on? That was the night I learned my lesson as he left the bar we were in at a pace of twenty miles per hour. I also learned that the day after, he moved towns. It was a harsh lesson learned. Never tell a man you love them first, they will go to extreme lengths to make you feel like an utter twat!

Linda exposed the outside as Aaron entered the room. I hoped it was Aaron anyway because there wasn't a weighty, bin man in sight. Quite the opposite in fact; he was of average height, blonde hair and eyes like aqua-marine crystals, so dazzling that he'd produced the effect of a glistening disco ball upon his presence in the room. 'Please let this be him,' I thought.

Linda opened the fridge and passed the hot-looking gentleman a can of lager. She whispered something in his ear and he started to approach me. This was one of those moments which I should have prepared for. I wasn't even wearing a Tena Lady. Aaron walked confidently over to me. I turned my head towards him, trying not to look desperate, even though those three words were screaming in my head. Fuck me now!

'Hi, it's nice to finally meet you. I'm Aaron.' He didn't even hold out his hand to greet me, he went straight for a kiss on the cheek. Where had this man been all my life? How the fuck had I never noticed him before? I planned to make an appointment at the opticians first thing Monday morning. I smiled by Aaron's kiss and I was quite positive that I was sweating.

'Nice to meet you Aaron, Linda has told me a lot about you.' Safe reply, I thought.

'I know, you think I'm some fat bin man don't you?' Replied Aaron. Oh shit! I glanced over to Linda, and squinted my eyes at her. This was possibly one of the most humiliating moments of my dating career. I knew that laughter was always a good way out of awkward situations.

'Ha, ha, ha, ha. Oh, Linda is so funny. I didn't say that – not in that way anyway. I said I bet he's some fat, fucking bin man.' I anticipated his response. Thank Christ, he laughed.

'You're funny. Linda said you were always up for a laugh.' Aaron seemed thrilled that I participated in witty banter. I rushed over to Linda.

'Hey Linda, he is the guy you were telling me about right? Please say it is.' I spoke quietly so only Linda would realise I was overly keen.

'Yes, he's the one. You said you weren't interested when I mentioned him the other day.' Linda was right, I did mention something along those lines. However, she did describe him in an unappealing way. Actually, her words were 'he empties bins for the Council, and is in his late forties.' Linda wasn't exactly a sales representative for potential cock, put it that way. I had to explain my interest...

'I'd fuck him senseless.' I was never diplomatic, especially if I'd not had any for a while.

'I knew you'd like him.' Linda appeared pleased with her cupid's aim.

'You described him as 'The Elephant man of the Council'. I was thrilled he wasn't!

Linda laughed. 'He's heavier than the last bloke you went out with.'

'By about two pounds.' I spoke and realised that Linda was judging me as a shallow woman. Maybe she was right – I had been around the track a lot through the summer season. Like the Grand Prix of dating, except I wasn't shagging Ferraris, I was riding the bangers. I accepted her judgement and walked sexily back towards Aaron.

For an hour we stood there like we were the only people at the party, discussing dating disasters and taking the absolute piss out of everyone in the room. He was like a male version of me on a sarcastic and witty level, however I had to explain a few things. Aaron was gorgeous, funny and charming but an intellect was something he was definitely not. I could live with that, nobody's perfect. Aaron and

I were so wrapped in one another's conversation that we didn't even notice that the other guests had left and Linda had fallen asleep on the couch. I was usually a very acute and observant person. Aaron had distracted me from everything that existed within a twenty-five metre square radius. This had never happened to me before – I was blown away by his ability to keep me from being nosey with the intricate goings on within a party atmosphere. I tried to smell my drink for rohypnol because this had never happened to me before.

Aaron and I continued our own private party back at my flat and before we knew it, the morning birds were singing. All night had been spent discussing anything and everything and I wasn't bored once. That was a first – being kept up all night without my knickers leaving my hips. It must have been love. Obviously I didn't say it this time, I wasn't a total moron. Aaron left that morning and within ten minutes he had sent a text message thanking me for a brilliant night.

What else can I say about Aaron Jones? One amazing night soon turned into weeks of incredible sex and copious amounts of laughter. No one had made me feel that way since Marcus. I was fuelled with love and excitement – I couldn't thank Linda enough for welcoming this man into my life. We were deeply in love and didn't care who knew or what they thought about it. My one regret with Aaron was listening to my heart. He moved in with me after weeks of being together. I would never have done this with anyone before but I was one hundred per-cent sure that I had found my soul mate and I had to grab this opportunity with both hands and make sure that Aaron was the one to permanently take the place on the left side of my bed.

The day Aaron moved in was an exciting one for me, despite warnings from friends and family. Helen was displeased and was worried about my state of mind, should it not work out. I spent days trying to reassure her that I was in love and he was the one. Typically, the explanation of Aaron's girth was the only thing that seemed to convince Helen.

Aaron didn't have many possessions, which I thought was sad, considering he was mid-forties. Amongst the boxes were a few books (picture ones), CD's, clothes and a gaming console. When Aaron unpacked his gaming console, he set it up without hesitation and connected it to my forty two inch plasma television, which was proudly placed on my breast wall. I was obviously baffled by this, who wouldn't be? I mean, a man of his age with a games console is bad enough, but he was setting it up on my television. My television, which was the bearer of my romantic comedy nights. My television, which kept me company on those accumulative nights in alone. Aaron completed the set-up and sat down on the sofa. He looked like the happiest man in the world; well he would be, my television was awesome and my couch was so comfortable that you'd take a piss on it if you could. Still, I looked on in sheer shock.

'What about the other boxes?' I asked pleasantly. Aaron shrugged his shoulders.

'It's fine babe, I'll sort them out tomorrow. Told my mate I'd be online tonight.' Aaron logged onto his account eagerly and put his feet up on my coffee table. What the fuck? It was our first night living together as a couple. Was he fucking serious? I was livid.

'Are you fucking kidding me, Aaron?' I swore with conviction. Aaron pulled his ridiculous headset off his head.

'What's wrong with you? This is the only hobby I have. I don't go out drinking anymore, I work hard and I've made a commitment to you. All I ask for is a few hours a day so I can play this game.' Aaron spoke in a rare tone. I walked into the kitchen to make a cup of tea. I lit up a cigarette and thought long and hard about the situation I had just gotten myself into. Was it too much to ask of him? I assumed it was a good thing that Aaron wasn't the type to go out drinking every weekend with his friends. It was a good thing that he believed that he was making a commitment to me. No one else ever had. Deliberation had got the better of me again and I concluded that I was going to try and make this relationship work. Surely it wasn't a bad thing that Aaron wanted to play his game? He wasn't abusive, disrespectful or impotent; maybe I was being too judgemental. I decided to apologise and give him the benefit of the doubt. I had my own little flaws and Aaron's were minor to the other incredible qualities, which were attributed to him.

After a while Aaron played the game less and less and we were beginning to make a comfortable life together. Every day consisted of sex and laughter. I was happy because they were my two favourite activities. Two glorious months passed by and he only seemed to play on the game for a couple of hours per day. I decided I could live with that. I could, until the newest edition of Extreme Marines was released. Imagine a child trying to get to sleep on Christmas Eve. The excitement builds upon them the closer Christmas morning approaches. They were the exact emotions expressed from Aaron. I was solemnly shocked when he left the flat to queue up at midnight, just so he could purchase the game with immediate intentions to play throughout the rest of the night. I'd like to think it was a joke when Aaron left the house in an Extreme Marines t-shirt and camouflage trousers – I shit you not! I also imagined all the gaming addicts queuing up for the game in a long line. Wouldn't that be the perfect opportunity to take an AK47 and kill the fuckers in one single attack?

Aaron played the new game for twelve hours solid. I walked into the living room with my morning brew and kissed him on the cheek, trying to show some support. Aaron's eyes were red, like he'd actually been to war and returned after a twelve month tour of Afghanistan. I took the controller from Aaron's hand and forced him to lie down on the couch. He fell asleep within minutes. I had to leave for work so I covered Aaron with a blanket and left. Aaron didn't need to work that day. He'd previously booked it off as a holiday, knowing that he would be held prisoner to the game for a whole night.

Whilst I was sat at my desk in work I was consumed with thoughts of Aaron and the impact the game had on him. The game had his attentions more than I could ever possibly dream of. Was it even rational to be jealous of a computer game? I spoke to a few work colleagues about the situation and found out that I wasn't the only Extreme Marines widow, there were millions of us worldwide suffering the same fate – a fate that we would never be priority as long as the product was still available on the market. I wanted to sob at my desk as reality smacked me straight in the nose. I had found a flaw in Aaron – something I thought was impossible a few months back.

I returned home from work that day and Aaron was sat back upright, controller in hand, screaming and shouting at the television as other online gamers participated in a game of fake war. The passion he held for the game could only be compared to watching Platoon on DVD, he genuinely thought he was making a difference for his Country. All I received that night was a smile and a nod to welcome me home. The flat was untouched and I even checked the side of the couch in case he had a piss bucket too.

Weeks had gone by since the release of the newest edition of that wretched game. I would be pottering around the house, listening to the sounds of guns, bombs and helicopters – I was beginning to think I had Gulf War Syndrome. One night he came to bed and started to get a bit raunchy. I turned my back to ignore him because I was pissed off through him neglecting me all day. He was overly persistent and tried to spoon me naked. I displayed zero interest.

'Hey come on, Roxy, what's wrong?' Asked Aaron, stupidly holding no understanding as to why I wasn't interested.

'I'm tired Aaron, I don't want to.' I wasn't tired, just fed up with being second place. Aaron kissed the back of my neck – he knew that would usually be enough for me to turn around and jump on him. Still, I held back and ignored him.

'Are you playing games with me?' He asked. I thought about it for a moment.

'Yes, I am actually, I am playing games. It's a new game called Extreme Vagina. You can play the new edition in six months, when it's released.' I was pleased with my retort.

Aaron sighed, rolled over and never spoke to me the rest of the night. At least I had some power as to when he did or didn't fire his weapon.

The day I decided to end things with Aaron was gut wrenching because we lived together. If I had taken a few months to date him without rushing into things and listening to my stupid heart then I wouldn't have been in that position. It was a conversation, which I'd held off for weeks but I couldn't go on any longer knowing that I was second to a games console and its shitty, fucking game. I decided to end things one particular day because it was my birthday. Instead of taking me out to wine and dine me he asked if it was ok if he could do it the weekend later – apparently it was double-points weekend. I looked on with confusion as he aimed the controller to shoot the animated, fictionalised soldiers. His expression was intense as he became top scorer in the pack he was apparently risking his life for. His win face resembled his come face. Sex would become mundane from that realisation, especially when he shot his weapon. I knew the best way to get Aaron's attention was to do the only thing, which I knew would instigate a full blown row and urge him to pack his minimal belongings. I unplugged the game at the wall, without giving him a chance to save it. Knowing his obsession, it was I who was being a brave soldier for once. Aaron jumped up from the couch, red-faced and ready to go into battle.

'What the fuck did you do that for?' Aaron was evidently angry. 'There was one minute left on that game. You stupid bitch!'

'It's over Aaron! Pack your stuff; take your stupid game and games console and fuck off.' I really didn't want to be so harsh but anyone who calls me a 'stupid bitch' is going to feel the extent of my hormones.

'Don't be so dramatic, Roxy, I haven't done anything wrong.' Replied Aaron, less angry yet deluded.

'That game is ruining your life,' I suggested.

'Don't talk stupid, Roxy, I had six lives left.' Aaron was serious. I had no choice but to place his pathetic little life into two boxes. I should have known that any man who has such a small amount of belongings has absolutely no life whatsoever. I guessed that was the reason why someone so funny and attractive was single. I doubt any rational woman would stand for his neglect, obsession and deluded attitude.

Aaron finally left that day. I left him with no choice as I put his boxes in the front garden. I told him that his care package had arrived just so he felt a bit more at ease leaving the flat. I cried for weeks after our break up. He was so close to proving that I can find happiness like other elite women. I too could have been happy with someone who made me laugh but still, that one essential flaw was enough to drive a wedge between us. It was his wedge though, in the shape of a games console. I vowed never to get involved with a gaming addict again and would warn any breathing woman to take that advice, no matter how desirable or funny the man may be.

I still remember one particular night with Aaron, when I was sat beside him on the couch. He was frantic at one of the other online players during a pretend game of war. Suddenly he shouted, loudly in my ear: 'You camping bastard.' Aaron was passionately loud, like someone had actually shot him in the leg, in real life. I frowned and glared at him confused and admittedly, slightly shaken. I asked him what he meant by 'camping bastard' as it was a term he used rather frequently. He explained it all to me. Apparently a camping bastard is when a player hides behind something in the game – like a sniper, instead of risking their lives like the other players. Thinking on, I still never understood why Aaron never joined the army in real life. He should join the army really, and go to Afghanistan – then we will see who the camping bastard is then!

Chapter 10

The Online Player

There are different ways to date a man, some which are positive and some which aren't. The probability of meeting someone worthy, depending on your standards and expectations, is intrinsically linked to where you meet them. For instance, if you meet a man in a library (like I did) you should expect to be dating an intellectual, geek or an escapee from a mental hospital. If you hang around golf clubs and cocktail bars, you can expect to meet a refined, wealthy type. Personally, I'd recommend loitering around some army barracks or become a volunteer at the fire station. The point I'm making is that there are so many more options other than visiting the same bars and meeting the same toss bags you end up enduring a three in the morning conversation with as he tries to persuade you to go back to his flat. When a man decides to chat you up before the closure of a night club, run for your fucking life; it's clear they just intend on having sex, even if they do bullshit you and tell you they have fancied you for years.

I was getting fed up of going out and visiting the same places, drinking wine and meeting the same players, losers, and worst of all ex-lovers. Helen mentioned that a woman from her works had just got married to a wealthy man who she'd met on an online dating site years before. Online dating was something I'd never ventured into before and I was curious to get involved. I thought it would be much easier and less awkward to type the words fuck off, pervert instead of actually saying it to their faces. As soon as Helen told me about it, I rushed home from work and logged onto my computer. I found a dating site called Keep Fishing and it was free! I set up my profile and spent four hours taking a decent photo of myself for my page. I thought that honesty was the best policy so I explained that I wanted to meet someone with the intention of marriage and forever after. A few weeks had gone by and I'd heard nothing. I sat down, had a re-think and changed my profile to 'looking for friendship and no-strings attached'. The day after I'd changed my profile I had forty messages in my inbox. I was amazed by how many men blatantly asked for sex. I had so many pictures of men's cocks that I could have created a collage – I had a lovely ten by eight frame I could have fit them all into. I was surprised to how many men claimed to be successful business men and millionaires. What the fuck were they doing on a free site then? I was prepared for the bullshitters – my extensive experience had taught me that. Out of all the messages I found one that was acutely interesting and showed potential. He complimented my photo, asked about my job and said he enjoyed quiet nights in curled up on the couch. He was thirty and liked the same type of music. I know from general flirting and dating that there aren't many men into heavy metal. Out of a perverted bunch, he was the only one who seemed interesting and normal. I messaged him!

His name was Adam Capello and he was an electrician (so he claimed). We spent quite a few evenings chatting online and I absolutely loved it! I would be late for work because we'd sit up till two in the morning discussing music, work and joking with each other. It was refreshing to feel a connection with someone without even meeting them. It was new territory for me and I wondered if I should have been doing this all along, instead of wasting my time and money getting pissed in bars and cringing as a sixty year old man hit on me. That's the worst for me. I'm not ageist whatsoever but when a man who's in his sixties asks where you have been all his life, I feel the urge to vomit bile and sweetcorn into his glass. Obviously I'd not been in his life that long because he was thirty years older. That's the type of shit I've had to put up with through zigzagging into the same watering holes, turning down the same men and watching my ex-partners try to be affectionate with their new girlfriends, for my benefit. Adam was nothing but a photograph with a virtual personality, which I prayed was genuine and he wasn't another fantasist who strung a few lines together to get his end away. Time would only tell as I arranged to meet him the following weekend. Luckily, he only lived five miles away.

Adam and I agreed to meet in the afternoon at a coffee house just on the outskirts of town. It was an uplifting change to meet someone over coffee instead of risking humiliation after a glass of wine too many – besides, my liver was in dire need of a detox. An added benefit of afternoon dating was that I could dress more casually, spend less time on hair and make-up and actually remember the conversation the day after.

When I arrived at the coffee house Adam was sat in a corner booth, he beckoned me over. As I approached him I was quite surprised because he certainly didn't look thirty, as it said on his profile. He looked at least forty. However, despite his endless wrinkles, I found him very attractive. Maybe he'd had a very stressful life? Maybe he was a heavy smoker, or maybe he was a sunbed addict who wasn't satisfied until he'd turned purple? Whatever reason, he possessed a very endearing smile and strikingly sexy brown eyes. I sat facing him.

'Thanks for coming; I wasn't sure you would turn up.' Spoke Adam.

'I was looking for somewhere to park, sorry. I would have let you know if I couldn't make it.' I looked as Adam pulled a box out of his pocket.

'I hope you don't think I'm being too forward but I already feel like I've know you for weeks. I brought you a little gift.' Adam spoke quietly as if he was embarrassed to be giving me a gift. I was taken back slightly because I wasn't expecting a gift so soon. I did shit myself for a split second in case he was a complete mentalist and had already bought me an engagement ring. I looked at him surprised by his gesture. I opened the box carefully.

'Aw, how sweet, you remembered.' I giggled softly. 'That's so sweet, thank you.' Adam had bought me a wine bottle stopper, made out of crystal. Whilst we were chatting online I used to explain how I could never get the cork back in the bottle so I felt obliged to drink the lot. I was thrilled with the gift, yet a little gutted that reality was that I should really cut down on my drinking. I put the wine stopper back into the box. 'Thanks so much for that, I love it. I do need to drink less. I'm so sorry, I didn't bring you anything.' I looked at his ageing face and thought that maybe I should have bought him a mirror.

'I didn't expect anything. I saw it the other day and thought of you and your alcohol problem,' Adam smiled. I was cringing.

'I am not an alcoholic!' I sternly replied.

'Really? You know the first sign of alcoholism is denial.' He was still grinning. I don't know what came over me but I whacked him on the side of his arm. In a playful manner of course, not in a psychotic way. I'd hit him like he was my best friend and a cheeky slap was allowed now and again. It suddenly hit me; we'd already made a huge connection online that I already felt like I knew him so well. I felt like I was dating a friend. I was considering becoming an ambassador for Keep Fishing – it was an innovative new approach for me and I was impressed by this way of meeting men. Adam rubbed his arm, exaggerating for sympathy.

'Whoa, I wouldn't like to really piss you off. What would you do if

I did, hit me with a feather next time?' Adam was clearly taking the piss but at least he accepted the slap as a jovial one.

The whole afternoon was lovely. We spent most of the time looking into one-another's eyes. Downside to dating someone online; you use up your conversation before you actually meet, however it gave us time to gaze and something was definitely happening between us. There was no weirdness or hesitation – I drove him straight back to my flat and we did it, right there, over the dining table. We couldn't even manage to walk to the bedroom. I was glad about that though, I was sure my rampant rabbit was sticking out of the bottom drawer. I can honestly say that I'd never had sex so spontaneously before but it felt like I'd been seeing him for weeks anyway. Adam wiped the perspiration from his forehead. It dripped so noticeably from his thick locks of blonde hair. The sex was amazing so I didn't want to ruin the moment by asking him his real age. Besides, if he was genuinely thirty and suffered with low-self-esteem then I would come across as a top-class bitch! The most important thing at the time was that I liked him, he made me laugh. If I had to pick a flaw at that time it would be that he wasn't extremely well endowed. I wasn't they type of girl to put a man down because of the size of his manhood and if he ever asked me about what I thought I would just explain that he has nothing to worry about – because the G-spot is only two inches in.

Weeks went by and before we knew it, we were officially a couple. There was no rush so we stuck to seeing one another twice a week. One weekday and one weekend day and night. He was busy conducting car deals and attending auctions and I was currently sucking up to impress my boss for the upcoming assistant manager's position. Life was relatively good at that point. Adam was enough to fulfil my needs and I enjoyed having my own space.

One unforgettable evening Adam came round and I spoiled him

to a palatable, fillet steak meal. I gave him the whole works, candles, red wine and oral. He'd had a long day at work and I was constantly topping up his glass when he wasn't looking. He wasn't a big drinker normally and I wanted to see what his personality was like once he'd a few too many. One ex-boyfriend only needed two pints of lager and he wanted to fight with anything that inhaled air. He was convinced that lager possessed the power of invincibility and every living-breathing creature should fear him. In a nutshell, he was an utter prick!

Adam was one of those tired drunks, which I soon found out as he collapsed onto my couch and showed no signs of response, even when I flicked his ears. He looked so peaceful so I covered him up with a fleece blanket and sat on the chair opposite him so I could watch him sleep. To be honest I got bored after two minutes and didn't want to turn on the television or it would have woken him up. I looked across on the arm of the couch and saw that his phone was flashing, yet there was no sound. It suddenly struck me that I never noticed Adam using his phone when he was with me, or if he did I wouldn't know too much as he obviously left it on silent all the time. I pondered for a moment as my mind began to wander. Pondering soon turned into an obsessive urge to grab his phone and check through it. I held the phone in my hand and thought carefully about the can of worms I could potentially open. There had been trust in our relationship, even though we'd only been together a few weeks. Then I thought about the other cheating fuck-wits I'd dated in the past and any thoughts of trust fell completely out of my head. 'Fuck it' I thought.

His phone was unlocked and I browsed through his applications. I saw his social networking page and clicked on the messages. I could have thrown up there and then on his sleepy head. He had messaged one girl telling her how great she looked when he saw her earlier.

Another message was just simply 'fancy a fuck?' My heart was racing to a dangerously fast beat and I felt physically unwell. That was just the social networking page. I browsed his Keep Fishing profile and he was romancing another thirty women as well as me. Granted he wasn't arranging to meet them all but it was clear that needle-dick loved every minute being online and trying to convince women he was this wonderful human being who loved quiet nights in and cuddles on the couch. It was the biggest heap of shit I'd ever read in my life. The worst of it was he'd updated his profile picture and I was stood in the background, in my flat. I could see the picture of my mother in the background hung on my wall. My only thoughts were 'cheeky, lying, sleazy, fucking lying, cheeky, fucking sleazy bastard'! Furthermore, I looked through his wallet and saw his driving licence. The lying scumbag's age was forty like I first thought. I wanted to launch his phone at the living room wall – I was so angry. I rationalised that my anger had gotten me in trouble in the past and my hastiness always resulted in deep regret.

Adam woke up shortly after, the glass of water poured over his head worked effectively. He sat up, shocked and wet.

'What the hell are you playing at, you bloody lunatic.' Adam was naturally angry. 'Seriously, what did you do that for?

'I don't know Adam, let me think!' I threw his phone at him with force, hoping to catch his genitals, although that would be a task. Adam's face couldn't have dropped anymore if he had had a stroke.

'What the fuck are you doing with my phone?' He was livid, but all men are once they've been rumbled. I held my composure.

'Normally, I would be ashamed of looking through someone's phone, Adam, but I'm bloody glad I did. You're disgusting. I'd like you to leave now!' I said rather calmly considering the circumstances. Adam placed his wet head in his hands.

'It's not what you think. I get mithered by the same girls all the time. I'm loyal to you.' Adam sounded pathetic in his attempt to try and bullshit me when I'd read messages that he'd sent that day.

'It's over Adam, I can't trust you now and I never will. You're a chaser, a player and a down right pervert. Oh and you're old as fuck!' He wasn't much older than me but I knew that his age bothered him or he wouldn't need to lie about it would he? I walked over to the front door and Adam shamelessly walked past me attempting one last lingering look. I looked right back at him into his eyes.

'Now fuck off!' I slammed the door just missing his heel as he left.

The experience with Adam taught me never to bother with online dating again. I was happy to have tried it; I'm an Aquarian, I'd try anything once. Like most of my other experiences, online dating was a learning curve and I wouldn't be able to trust anyone who was so besotted by receiving that much attention from other women, online or not! I wouldn't mind though, it wasn't as if I didn't put out, spoil him and give him his space. The girls he spoke to were of average standard. I imagined their user names would be 'missgullible,' Iloveliars,' or 'desperateforanything'. I felt anguish for these poor, mistaken ladies who would fall for his hogwash. They had no idea they were about to be used. However, if they can be stupid enough to believe he was thirty of age when his profile picture clearly displayed a man who looked in his forties then I guess these girls were as equally as desperate as he was for attention, like myself previously and shamelessly. His profile and obsession to receive compliments from younger women did confirm that he was having a mid-life crisis. When he was at mine he would spend a good ten minutes in the mirror, stretching out the lines on his face yet through his own delusions, he would smile at what he saw. I'd smile too, purely because he reminded me of my father.

Chapter 11

The Narcissist

I wasn't always a fixated sceptic in my quest for love. When I meet a prospective boyfriend these days I am weary but obsessed with finding flaws they may possess. Sure, I'd love to meet a man completely flawless but realistically I know this is an impossibility. I am riddled with flaws myself. I'm slightly high maintenance, I like my own space, I can express too much sarcasm and anger when I'm in that mood and I'll openly admit that my main defect is looking for flaws in men. Granted I've been in love and had my heart broken a couple of times but when you've had a really bad experience with someone in your younger years, that person sets the wheels in motion for all future relationships. A relationship so convoluted that you will do anything to protect yourself from ever letting something so psychologically damaging visit your life again.

When I was only eighteen years old I dreamed of meeting the right man, settling down, having a family and living a life of harmonious joy. Of course at eighteen years old I was still immature myself and unsure what to expect once I had fallen in love. At the time I was just besotted with the idea of being a Princess, maybe my mother had told me too many fairy tales when I was a young child. Gullibility is a given when you're eighteen years old and only the unlucky girls of that age will be unfortunate enough to find a man with the biggest flaw and worst personality of them all; that man is a narcissist.

If you ever meet a man who is good looking, associated with

influential people, show no remorse or gratitude for anything you have done for them or have the inability to apologise then chances are you have found yourself a narcissist. If such a person, through a cruel twist of fate enters your life then all I can suggest is run. Run for your fucking life. Running could save your heart, mind and permanent well being. Maybe I didn't run fast enough or soon enough and now I suffer a life seeking out possible ways of not being with someone because the slightest thing they do pisses me off. Usually I have good reason to end the relationship or flee from a first date but maybe it was the narcissist who imprinted so many irrational fears into my head? One thing I can thank him for, I'm no doormat these days. The closest a man gets to wipe his feet on me is if we are playing some kinky sex game.

I met Zac Cameron at a local pub when I was only eighteen years old. I was ridiculously nervous because I'd just started to go out drinking with my friends and was apprehensive of older women who used to look at me and my friends like we were the future generation of husband stealers. In the defence of my friends and I, we did look much better than the women in the local pubs and it wasn't our fault that their husbands were undressing us mentally with their perverted eyes.

One night I won't ever forget is when I was approached by a handsome man, blatantly older than me. Not much older but not too old to class the meeting as father and daughter. I never forget the night when he approached me.

'Wow,' he gasped. 'You are the best looking girl ever to set foot in this place.' I blushed like a twelve year old girl who had just received her first kiss. 'I'm Zac.'

'Roxy,' I replied. I wasn't a girl of many words back then. Zac stared right into my soul; my unwise, naïve soul with not enough life experience. He was incredibly attractive and groomed to faultlessness.

'Can I buy you and your friends a drink?' Asked Zac. My friends began to nudge me like a pack of wolves salivating for alcohol. We weren't career girls at the time and would use baby sitting money to buy a few halves at the weekend.

'Thank you, if you don't mind?' I was a hopeless flirt.

'I don't mind at all. It's not often I get to treat a lovely young group of girls. It's my pleasure.' Zac showed no hesitation in opening up his wallet, which was deliberately opened wide so my friends and I could see the extent of his wealth. I was so impressed that I was already imagining myself sat outside his villa whilst he brought me fruitful treats and beverages as I happily soaked up the warmth from the sun. Zac ordered three drinks at the bar and passed them over singularly to my friends and me, offering each of us a glorious smile.

'I've never seen you in here before, do you live locally?' Zac looked optimistic.

'I do, I live a few streets away actually.' I was still very shy but still managed to notice Zac's eyes light up with excitement.

'Wonderful, I'm only a few minutes' walk away myself. That's lucky isn't it?' I was the lucky one. I'd never been approached by a real man before. I was always hit on by lads my own age who thought that a good fingering behind a tree on the football field was their height of romance. Zac didn't look like the fingering type. He looked like the type to wine and dine a young girl, lavishing her with gifts and make love to her like in the films. My stomach actually turned by the thought of sleeping with an older man. What if I wasn't experienced enough? What if he was too big for me to handle? The thoughts terrified me yet I was mesmerised by his generosity, looks and charm.

Zac walked me home that night, gripping my hand as if I was the only person who mattered to him in the world. I didn't want him to ever let go. He impressed me with stories of his achievements. He almost made the Olympic team for the javelin and he just missed out being a professional footballer because he'd broken his tibia in three places just before he signed the contract. He left me at the door of my parent's house and kissed my hand like a perfect gentleman. I climbed into bed that night completely elated that this wonderful man, who I'm sure I was already in love with had chosen me. The fact that he was ten years older made no difference, he didn't look much older anyway.

Zac spent the next two months taking me out and he always allowed me to choose where I wanted to go. At the time, I was a cinema lover and needed to watch every film that was released. I also liked to go roller skating but I didn't want to look like a complete child so I never confessed my roller habits. Zac worked in a bank and there was no hesitation in inviting me along to parties and family gatherings. His friends were all in high powered jobs and earned more money than I could ever dream of possessing in a lifetime. I was getting ready to start my marketing degree at university and Zac would proudly inform his colleagues and friends that he was in love with a university girl. He always praised me for my intelligence and ambition, he made me feel like I could do anything.

I'll never forget the moment on my first day of university when Zac gave me a velvet box to open. I'd hoped it was a ring but what was revealed was equally as uplifting and made me ecstatic with happiness. Zac had given me a key to his plush apartment and asked me to move in with him. At eighteen years old this was a dream come true. I always thought I'd have to kiss a few frogs before I settled down but didn't care that I didn't need to, being with Zac was the only place I wanted to be for the rest of my life.

I'd been living with Zac for two weeks and I sat at home in his apartment waiting for him to return from work. He'd always return home about six but this night it was ten and I was becoming increasingly worried. When he eventually arrived home at midnight I was relieved that nothing had happened to him. He had been drinking because I could smell the lager on his breath before he had even got close enough to speak to me.

'Zac, I was worried sick, where have you been?' I spoke and he ignored my question and scanned the room with his tired eyes.

'How fucking lazy are you?' He sniped. I looked to where he was looking but I was still confused.

'What do you mean?' I regretfully asked. Zac pointed to the kitchen, I looked.

'There, fucking pots. I don't want to come home to a shithole every night. I've worked hard for this apartment. People would kill to be able to afford a place like this.' Zac expressed a frightening anger that I had never witnessed in the months we'd been together. I looked back in the kitchen and there was one plate and one mug – everywhere else was spotless.

'I'll wash them now, it won't take a minute.' I was shaken by the magnitude of his anger over two small pots.

Zac continued his rant. 'There are loads of women who would love to be where you are now. Do you know how many women I turn down on a weekly basis to be with you?' I didn't know and the thought of it made me sick. I felt bad because I'd clearly angered him.

'I'm sorry, Zac, it won't happen again. I didn't realise. I love you.' I walked over to him hoping to have my sincere apology accepted. He stood there, silent like I'd just murdered his mother or committed a crime of that level. I threw my arms around him and gave him a loving hug. I felt no reciprocation. It was like hugging a shop mannequin but the mannequin expressed more emotion. I looked down and instead of putting his arms around me; Zac placed his hands into his trouser pockets.

I barely slept that night wondering what I had done that was so wrong. I was perplexed and my only rationalisation was that maybe Zac had one drink too many and tiredness had taken over. He did work really hard.

The next morning Zac had gotten up early and left for work. I sat by the phone all day waiting for an apology for his unacceptable behaviour. My mum was the only person who rang all day. Surely, a man with such wonderful manners like he expressed upon our first meeting would have the natural ability to apologise? Not Zac and from then on I was confused as to where that lovely, charming man had gone who I fell in love with months before. Being such a young, vulnerable age I only wanted to do things to please him, anything so I wouldn't have to experience the Zac who surfaced that night simply over a mug and a plate.

It was my nineteenth birthday and Zac had arranged a party at our apartment. He'd invited all his friends and my friends and had the apartment decorated with pink balloons, decorated tables, a cocktail bar and bottles of champagne. I returned home from university and felt completely overwhelmed by his grand gesture. I was also confused because he'd ignored me for weeks, unless he wanted sex of course. I'd been ignored because I'd burnt his toast one morning before he went to work. I returned home with a bag, which held my new dress. Zac had given me some money to buy a dress he'd seen in a designer shop the week before. On my arrival home I was thrilled by the efforts he had put in to make my birthday special. Maybe he wasn't angry with me anymore, it was only a piece of toast after all. I showed my honest gratitude to Zac for his valid efforts.

'Oh Zac, the apartment looks beautiful. Thanks so much for this.' Zac walked over to me and kissed me on the forehead.

'Well, it is your birthday, Princess.' I belonged to him again. 'Did you buy that dress I told you to get?' I held up the bag and shook it in front of him. 'Good, hurry up and put it on, I want to see you in it before our friends arrive.'

I rushed into the bedroom following a high speed shower and slipped on the dazzling, black dress Zac had paid a fortune for. I pinned up my hair in an elegant fashion and wore minimal make up. Zac hated me to wear lots of make up; he said it made me look too fake. Zac shouted to me.

'You ready yet, they'll be arriving in a minute!' I was so flattered that he wanted to spend a few moments with me before our friends arrived. I touched up my hair, brushed down the dress and walked out of the bedroom in the skit of a catwalk model. I felt amazing. Zac's jaw hit the floor.

'What the fuck are you wearing?' I looked down at my dress.

'The dress you told me to buy. What's the problem?' I was confused.

'It's black! I told you to buy the one in red.' His tone was becoming louder.

'It's the exact same dress, Zac, just in black. They didn't have my size in red.' I felt terrified and wasn't sure what to say to make things better.

'Maybe you should try losing a bit of weight then you would have been able to fit into the red one.' Zac turned and started to check his hair in the wall mirror. I was still bemused as I was only a size ten. I wanted to cry but he hated it when I cried. I cried when my Mum's dog died and he told me to 'get a fucking grip'. Since then I cried alone when he was at work. Zac continued with his annoyance.

'Look at me; I've made a huge effort to look good for your birthday. My friends are going to think I'm living with a scrubber.' Zac's harsh words instigated a rare defence mechanism within me. He was never like this in front of my friends and certainly not his friends. I couldn't take it anymore and I was convinced that as soon as someone knocked at the door, he would be loving Zac again – one who doted on his lady and was the centre of attention. I felt an epiphany there and then and I'd finally worked out the motives of this monster that I had the unfortunate naivety of falling in love with. I might have only been turning nineteen but I knew my self worth. I wanted to teach this controlling, hideous prick a harsh lesson so I turned my phone on to record the conversation.

'Why are you always nasty to me when we are alone, Zac?' This was the first sign of bravery I had shown.

'Why? Because you're a fucking idiot. You think you're fucking awesome because you're doing a degree. So what? When you've achieved as much as I have I might just have a little bit more respect for you.' His true colours were pouring out like a multiple paint spillage in a DIY shop. I continued to deliberately play the victim.

'I try so hard for you, Zac. I can't do anything right in your eyes. I love you so much, why don't you tell me that from time to time?' I replied with the whiniest voice I could act on. Zac was developing another rage as I predicted.

'Why would I continuously tell you that I love you when I don't?' He began to unravel. 'Truth is I wanted a cleaner who would open her legs for me just in case I didn't pull at the pub. I knew you were stupid enough to do it because you're weak and pathetic.'

There was a knock at the door and I put my phone in the nearest drawer. Zac answered and Jekyll had quickly returned.

'Mick,' welcomed Zac. 'Alright pal, thanks for coming.' Zac looked at me. 'Roxy love, Mick's here.' I walked over to Mick and he gave me a kiss on the cheek.

'Happy Birthday, Roxy,' said Mick thoughtfully. 'You look stunning.' Zac smiled at Mick.

'Doesn't she just. She's a diamond.' Said Zac.

Mick admired my dress. 'That's a posh dress, must have set you back a bit, Rox.' Zac spent no time in jumping in.

'I bought it for her. Tell him how much I paid, Roxy?' Zac was obsessed with letting people know how much he'd spent on every single item. The wonderful Zac, who was generous, caring and so loving to his girlfriend. I was actually embarrassed to honour Zac's request so I changed the subject.

'Would you like a drink, Mick?' I felt a tiny bit of glory as Zac struggled to hide his anger.

'That'd be lovely, Roxy; I'll have a can of lager if there's one going.' Replied Mick. I walked over to the fridge and passed Mick a cold can of lager. Zac was at the door as more of our friends entered the apartment. I cringed as Zac charmed every single woman who passed through. He loved every minute of it and from that moment I realised that the party was for him, not me. I meant absolutely nothing to him unless I could assist him in looking good in front of other people. My job was done and I was ready to leave – not before I had my revenge of course.

Zac was in the corner of the room singing on the karaoke machine, gyrating to his female work colleagues, who flocked around him like they were at an Elvis Presley concert. I wasn't even jealous anymore – if any of them were unfortunate enough to become his next victim then there was no room for jealousy. I was sincerely afraid for them that no one should have to endure the mental torture that I was subjected to. Following Zac's rendition of Heartbreak Hotel, he began to make an announcement on the microphone.

'Roxy, can you come up here, please?' Zac was breathless from all the singing and dancing. I obliged his request for my own pleasure to unfold.

'Coming, darling,' I skipped over in hyperbolic happiness. I kissed Zac and forced a fake smile as he pulled me into his chest, repeatedly kissing my forehead. Our friends were all looking on.

'You all know how much I love this woman and how much effort

I've put in to make her nineteenth birthday a special one...' Zac was savouring the applause. He continued...

'It's been almost a year since we met and I'd like to say in front of everyone that it's been one of the best years of my life.' I was shocked as to how Zac could fool all these people so well. The guests applauded and began to chant...

'Speech, speech!' This was perfect timing. I held up my mobile phone, much to Zac's confusion and put my mouth to the microphone.

'I just wanted to say thank you all for coming, it's been lovely to see you all here on my birthday. I'm so grateful, I really am.' They applauded again. That was the genuine bit done for the guests and now for the unravelling of a monster. 'Zac, you have made such a difference to my life, even when I don't deserve it.' My sarcastic tone was becoming more apparent. Zac's expression was one of puzzlement. I continued. 'I'd like everyone to raise their glasses for my boyfriend, Zac, who makes a massive effort to make me feel different every day.' Everyone held up their drinks.

'To Zac.' I looked right into Zac's confused eyes and placed my mobile phone against the microphone.

'Zac, you have been sooooo good to me that I decided it was about time our friends knew how well you treated me and how I deserve everything.' I pressed play on the recorder as our previous argument began to play loudly against the microphone. The message was only a minute long but definitely enough to reveal Zac as a despicable human being who had fooled everybody in the room. Zac squirmed in the corner of the kitchen as every female in the room scowled at him. His male friends held their heads in shame and some began to walk out of the apartment.

I grabbed my handbag and headed for the front door. Some of the guests were offering sympathetic glances and some hadn't moved due to the shock of Zac's real ego being divulged. I took one last look at Zac who looked like stone in the corner. His life was ruined for now. For the first time through our time together I actually felt like a narcissist, because for the first time I felt no remorse.

Chapter 12

Girl Talk

I haven't had a single date for six months and I am absolutely fine with it. It is, however my thirty eighth birthday and I've woken up feeling like old lady spinster destined to live a life of solitary confinement, absorbed by my couch whilst I hold lengthy conversations with myself over tea and digestives. I leaned over to check my legs for varicose veins and looked over to my bedside table at my one gift, which my mother had dropped off the day before. All I could think about was how there was nobody to wake up beside me. Turning thirty eight wasn't something that occupied me with delight and I had no urge to cartwheel the room due to the shit life I was leading. Being single on my birthday is doubly disappointing because today is Valentine's Day. Having a special someone in my life was good on my birthday because I reminded them that they had to buy me two lots of gifts. I would always put my birthday cards in the window but realise that because it was Valentine's Day and that it probably gave off the impression that I was a bit of a slag. I always felt like I was destined to be married before I was forty and to find my soul mate and marry them within two years was becoming more distant. Like my nipples. I was permeated in self pity but a knock at the door restored my hopes of a new beginning. You never know what's around the corner, that's what people say. One door closes and another one opens. I'm impatient and an opportunist. I don't open doors; I kick the fucker in with steel, toe capped boots.

I threw on my dressing gown to prevent my poor visitor from having recurring flashbacks, which would haunt them till their dying breath and I opened the door. There was a delivery man stood before me holding up a beautiful bouquet of white roses. White roses are my favourite flower and whoever sent them obviously knew this about me – I hoped from an admirer. Fuck it, I'd even accept them from one of my ex's, I would consider that one last time for old time's sake. I took the flowers and closed the door because I couldn't wait to rip open the card and see which gentleman had kindly sent me my favourite flowers on my birthday. I opened the card, which read *Wishing you a very happy birthday. Love you lots. See you later. Helen xx*. Don't get me wrong, I love Helen and I love the flowers but I couldn't help but fight that one tear that tries to fall when you feel inherently gutted. The card did remind me that the girls were coming to mine that evening to celebrate my birthday, indoors at my request.

I spent four hours cleaning. The only time my flat received a thorough clean was when I had guests coming round. I hate it when people unexpectedly turn up when the place looks like a teenager's bedroom and there's nothing worse than a guest visiting the bathroom when your knickers are on the bathroom floor – I've lost count of how many times that has happened to me, yet still I leave them on the floor. Knowing I was expecting guests gave me plenty of time to hide the knickers, sex toys and present myself as an independent woman who thrived on cleaning and was coping with her single life. It's utter bullshit but there's nothing wrong with faking it once in a while.

The clock approached seven and I could hear my friends chanting 'Happy Birthday' as they approached the front door. I opened the door to a sea of arms, which fought to hug me first. I received more kisses in those few seconds than I ever had in a lifetime – it felt good to know that my nearest and dearest were prepared to bring me out of my pit of despair and revitalise my hopes and dreams of eternal happiness and that my long term partner would never suffer with impotence or premature ejaculation.

I situated my living room so the chairs were circled around my huge coffee table, which now, thanks to my friends was covered with various alcoholic beverages and the most calorific snacks they could find. Helen was here, checking that I'd actually put the flowers in a vase. She loved a get together, especially at my house – she knew she didn't have to clean. I hoped she didn't over indulge because the last time she drank at mine she hurled in my bathroom sink and left it there for me to clean. I couldn't have a party without her there, she was my oldest friend.

Tania sat opposite me, happily pouring me a glass of the finest white. I'd known Tania for fifteen years. We met in a factory we worked in together and discovered that we shared the same love for music and the same disregard for men. That was until she finally met the love of her life, Michael. Tania was an inspiration for me as she too was a social lingerer who was unfortunate to meet hapless losers who never met her expectations. Michael changed her views forever. They have a relationship that the best movie writer couldn't create. She is one of those people who will give you the harshest truth whether you want to hear it or not. She was notorious for her slap when any of us made bad decisions regarding men. With my track record I'm surprised I don't look like I suffer with rosacea. A tattooed princess with an edgy personality that when she spoke her mind even Satan would run into the darkest depths of hell.

Michelle was sitting beside me chatting to Helen as I accepted my first glass of birthday wine from Tania. Michelle was one of the quieter ones of the group. Sweetness personified her and she's one of those people you couldn't be angry with even if you tried really hard to slightly speak out of turn. Michelle was a creative girl who could turn the shittiest piece of furniture into a marvellous creation worthy of a high street furniture shop. She was very much like me when it came to choosing Mr Wrong. Her dating record exceeded mine by a mile; however she was clued up and refused to settle for anything but the best. A raven haired beauty that could lure the sexiest men in the club just by exposing her smile. Personally, I think her double G breasts had something to do with it. I'd only known Michelle for a few years but felt blessed to have her amongst my circle of friends – besides she listened to my crap long enough, probably because she understood the trials and tribulations of dating.

Joanne was happily consuming her third glass of wine. I'd never known a girl who could drink so much and wake up the next morning with no hangover, this sickened me. She was the only girl I knew who really didn't give a shit about finding a life partner. She was recently divorced and embraced the single life like every day and every man was her last. She's a fluent party girl who loves nothing more than a glass of wine and bloody good laugh. I desperately wished I could ingest her attitude regarding the single life.

Amongst my other friends was Amber – a survivor of breast cancer and a wholly spirited person whose motivation and integrity was inspiring for all of us. Heather was a science teacher and through the short time I'd known her she was completely supportive with every decision I made, even the bad ones. Gillian was the one whom I called my 'posh friend' because she spoke so eloquently. She was a super charged business woman who worked consistently, juggling married life and three children. Emma arrived with the girls and I was glad she came because she always laughed at my ridiculous jokes. It was good to have her here because I've never known anyone go on more holidays and trips than her. Actually, I think she was flying out in the morning. Debra was another one of my dear friends who I rarely saw due to her busy work schedule and the fact that she finally found her happy ending. I missed her company so I was thrilled that she came to support my impending approach to forty. Karen was my university friend who could turn any man's head on any given day. A thoughtful, intelligent girl who always offered a friendly, sympathetic ear to – I tugged on her ears often. Kim and Yvonne came together as they live a few doors away from one another. They appreciated a night away from their children and were always up for a good laugh, usually at me and my stories of disastrous dating. Then there's Nina – a lady with an enormous heart and personality. There wasn't a party without her and her hilarious analogies on life.

Helen stood up holding up her glass of wine. 'Right everyone, I'd just like to wish Roxy a very happy birthday.' Everyone stood and held up their glasses. I forced a smile at the collective reminder that I was ageing without love.

'Thanks for reminding me girls – much appreciated,' I responded sarcastically. Michelle gave me a hug.

'It's not that bad, Roxy, you look great for your age.' Michelle meant well. 'We could still go out tonight if you want to?'

'No thanks, babe. Really, I'm really happy that you all came here. You lot are all I need tonight.' I meant it too. 'I've just not been that bothered about going out lately, I think I've lost my mojo.'

'It's probably in your knicker drawer,' shouted Helen. She would know because I've never known a woman who owned so many sex toys. She and Scott had an incredible sex life but it was never enough for Helen, she indulged in many afternoon private sessions with her 'toys'.

'Have you heard from Adam since?' Asked Tania.

'Have I fuck,' I replied. 'He'll be online luring some poor, deluded girl into a false sense of love and security.'

'Poor and deluded, like you were?' Retorted Tania. She was right –

I did rush into that one a bit too hastily.

'Fuck him, anyway,' shouted Nina. 'There are plenty more sharks in the sea.' We all laughed, mainly because we knew all about each other's dating records. Some of us were still piling up the records – mine will end up in some large warehouse due to the lack of room. Tania, in usual style began to top up everyone's glass.

'I reckon we should all share our biggest dating disasters to cheer Roxy up. Who's in?' Asked Tania. The girls expressed different looks from eager to weary. Michelle didn't seem keen.

'How would that cheer her up? And, I've not really had any that bad and if anything, Roxy will be depressed.' Michelle was very private and sometimes it took a lot of prodding to get any information out of her.

'I could tell you stories, which would turn your stomach, Roxy,' chirped Deb. 'I know Emma has had a few she'd like to forget, hey Emma?' Deb nudged Emma in the arm, which forced a glare from Emma to suggest near death if Deb exposed any of her secrets.

'Oh Deb, don't be silly, my dating record would send Roxy to sleep, not cheer her up.' Emma responded hoping the focus would shift elsewhere.

'Brilliant idea, I'll start,' said Helen. 'The worst date I ever had was when I was eighteen. This lad asked me out at college and said he wanted to take me somewhere special. I got really excited and dressed up really nice for him. He took me to a lovely Italian restaurant and guess what?' We all waited in anticipation. 'He told me that he had a small cock.'

'Fuck off!' Muttered Amber. 'Why would he tell you that?'

Helen continued, 'Well, apparently he was embarrassed about it and said that if he was up front about it then the girl wouldn't be too disappointed.' Kim scratched her head.

'So, did you shag him then?' Kim gulped her wine, waiting anxiously for Helen's reply.

'Well, yes. After he told me, I had to see it for myself.' Helen started to giggle to herself.

'Was it as tiny as he said?' Asked Amber.

'Hmm, how can I explain it?' Helen paused for thought and began to giggle. 'Let's just say, I didn't know if I was being fucked or fingered.' Michelle spat out her wine in shock. We all laughed together and watched Helen as she wiggled her little finger to emphasise his boyhood. Michelle seemed bewildered.

'But he was only eighteen. Don't men finish growing when they are twenty one?' We laughed again, much to Michelle's disapproval. 'I'm being serious!'

'Ok, who's next? What about you Joanne?' Asked Tania. Joanne sat back and we could see the itinerary of men running through her head like a mini movie.

'Hang on, this could take a while girls.' I loved to wind Joanne up. 'She's spoiled for choice.'

'Piss off,' interrupted Joanne. 'There are a few that's all. I'm just trying to make my mind up which one was the worst... Oh, I have one.' Joanne opened another bottle of wine and started to top up her glass. 'Ok, I met this lad on a dating site. Don't judge me, I was skint and it was the only way I could meet men at the time.'

'It can't be as bad as my disaster with Adam,' I blurted.

'Oh yes it can, Roxy.' Joanne continued with her story. 'This guy was listed on the site claiming he was a wealthy accountant with a massive cock. I couldn't understand why a rich man with a massive cock would need to even go on a dating site...'

'Because they're all boring bastards,' exclaimed Yvonne. Joanne nodded in agreement and continued with her date story.

'I met up with him because I was intrigued and curious. You'll be surprised that I've never actually been with anyone who was over

120

six inches.' Joanne began to chuckle to herself. 'You'll love this, Roxy. When I arrived on the date he was only just over five feet tall – I had my six inch heels on and we looked ridiculous stood together. I spent the whole night walking bare foot so people wouldn't point and stare so much.'

'Why didn't you just leave?' Asked Deb.

'Well, I wanted to but I needed to see that cock.' Joanne had almost finished a full glass of wine whilst telling her tale. 'I went back to his house, which was gorgeous by the way. We got naked and I looked down at his bits and it didn't look any bigger than any other I'd seen.'

'So he lied to you to get you into bed?' Asked Kim

'No, he genuinely believed that his manhood was really huge.' Insisted Joanne.

'But why?' Kim was insistent. 'Did he have bad eyesight?' Joanne smirked at Kim and put her glass on the table.

'It was because he had small hands.' Explained Joanne. We all vented our response with loud laughter.

'Did you not bother then?' Asked Kim.

'No, I still shagged him, I'd already got undressed.' Joanne said it like it was the most natural thing in the world. We all loved her for her blatant honesty when it came to sex and men. I could never imagine her settling down, she absolutely loved her single endeavours, small cock or not. We all looked around at one another wondering who was next to divulge their darkest secrets. Michelle raised her hand.

'I've got one for you.' We all looked at Michelle, curious as to what possible story she had been keeping from us for all these years. The quiet one was finally opening up and we waited with intense expectation. Luckily, Michelle had had quite a few drinks by now so it was easier for her to be rude and amusing for us to see. She began her tale.

'I met this guy whilst I was shopping believe it or not. He was in the supermarket and I was struggling to reach some discounted wine. He saw me struggling and walked over. He was over six feet tall so he didn't even have to stretch.' Michelle took a deep breath.

'What's wrong,' I asked. Michelle placed her hand on her chest.

'It makes me queasy when I think about it.' Michelle exhaled. 'Ok, you know what I'm like with hairy men.'

'What's wrong with hairy men? Asked Heather. 'I love a man who has a hairy chest – one that I can run my fingers through at night, before I go to sleep.'

'Yuk!' Muttered Michelle. 'This is much worse, Heather. After a few dates, we finally got around to the bedroom bit.' We all looked at one another and smirked, Michelle could never bring herself to use expletives so 'bedroom bit' meant shagging to us. Michelle rolled her eyes at us all, knowing we were taking the piss. 'Let me finish! Ok, so he took off his shirt and he had the hairiest back I'd ever seen. I wanted to spew on him. I had to go through with it because he would think I was shallow.'

'So did you not see him again after that?' Asked Heather.

'Yes, I did actually.' Michelle sniggered to herself. 'I really liked him so I offered to cook him a nice meal and invited him round to my flat. I promised to give him a massage at the end of the night.'

Heather expressed confusion. 'But why would you give him a massage if you hated his hairy back so much?' Michelle sniggered once more.

'Ah, you see I was a bit naughty. I gave him a massage using hair removal cream. He flipped at me and that was the end of that.' Michelle's story united us all with laughter, especially as she is the one who we wouldn't expect that type of behaviour from. Nina chirped in the laughter.

'I feel your pain, Michelle. I gave a blow job to a man who was so hairy, that afterwards I had to go to the bathroom and shave my teeth.' Nina's comment extended the jovial atmosphere, to the point of stomach cramps and shakes. This was the most perfect birthday for me. Tania's idea of exposing our dating mishaps were the perfect way to make me feel at home and I wasn't the only woman who suffered many losses through continuously acquainting myself with the biggest prats our town had to offer.

The end of the night consisted of a large group of highly intoxicated friends. The evening couldn't have gone better and despite my mid morning woes, I was thankful to have so many wonderful friends in my life. I realised that I would never be alone and crazy, cat lady wasn't an option anymore. My man was out there somewhere and if I have to endure a few more dating mishaps then so be it – at least it will be a humorous topic of conversation to amuse my dearest friends.

Chapter 13

Mrs Wrong

When I need to readdress my life, I like to have a long, hard think about what I'm doing and where I'm going. I like to sit in a darkened room, which is illuminated by scented candles with the sound of love songs playing in the background. Not those songs that choke you with everlasting love but those songs written by bitter singers who have been dumped or wronged by men in their lives. Those songs that make you think 'fuck you, I'm moving on' and motivate you knowing that there is another life after you've had your heart ripped out by some lying, cheating, abusive shagwit. Following my birthday, I was really enlightened to welcome a fresh me; one who wanted to pursue my true love, even accepting the odd flaw as long as it was just a little one. I believe in positive thinking and if you ask the universe for help and expose your positivity then you should expect a return with something positive. It's like karma. I know that one day the people who wronged me will get their comeuppance. It wasn't ever necessary for me to seek revenge. Hatred is an emotion I don't wish to have so I spend time meditating and pushing all negativity out of my ageing body. It was a bit of a struggle getting rid of the bitterness though.

I think that time alone is essential, especially when you are at a crossroad in your life. I had two choices; hide away in my flat why other women went out and bagged the last of the good men or reinvent my attitude and try and meet someone who met my expectations and treated me the way I deserved to be treated. I'm not high maintenance but I do believe that if I treat my man to the highest extent of my kindness then I expect nothing less in return! I've put in enough years of dating – it was about time I retired and settled with someone who not only possessed the looks of an Italian but someone who was kind, considerate and was accustomed to sex about ten times a week. He was out there somewhere but I'm afraid that my previous endeavours have left me with a hazy view of ever finding someone compatible with my requirements.

I booked myself a day's holiday from work to pamper myself with birthday money left by my wonderful family and friends. I'd booked myself into a spa at a luxurious hotel. This is something I desperately needed to get my head together and contemplate my future. I will not be alone and I will meet a wonderful man who loves me for who I am and possess the sexual skills of a porn star. That was my daily mantra when I sent out positive thoughts to the universe.

I arrived at the plush hotel and booked myself in at the reception. The receptionist passed me a beautiful, fluffy white robe and spa slippers, which I intended to take home with me. Part of my new regime was to exercise more. I've dropped a few pesky pounds so I treated myself to a new bikini with the acceptance of age and my body was what it was. I didn't look too bad considering I was thirty eight. My backside resembled a road map through stretch marks but I am a new woman who is embracing age and life, with the notion that anything could happen on any given day. Helen always blurted on that life is too short and I was finally taking that concept on board and grabbing life by the bollocks.

I entered the pool area and smiled with ease because it wasn't too busy. It's so hard to relax when there are too many swimmers and old ladies in pairs, discussing the latest bargains on the market. I walked straight over to the Jacuzzi, stepped in and began my day of relaxation.

My head was resting on the edge of the Jacuzzi and my eyes were closed so I could absorb the silence and immerse myself with my positive thoughts. I must have had my eyes closed for about ten minutes because I never realised that someone else had climbed into the Jacuzzi. I rubbed the water from my eyes and looked up. The universe had answered my constructive thoughts. A dark haired man with amazingly green eyes was sat opposite me, smiling and looking incredibly hot! I instantly felt the self conscious devil tapping me on the shoulder as I remembered that I was wearing a bikini, which exposed the road map that is my arse and I wasn't wearing any make up. This was both the universe's way of sending me the man of my dreams, like I asked or it was playing a cruel game and laughing at my facial nakedness. The man smiled at me.

'Hi, have you come here alone?' I'm sure he was enquiring whether or not I was single. I may look like a bare faced prune but I know damn well when a man is trying to weigh me up.

'I am yes.' I was glad I was alone. I think I was blushing too – at least that would brighten up my pasty face. 'I'm Roxy.' His face expressed approval of my name.

'Nice to meet you, Roxy, I'm Mike.' He spoke with a delightful, calming tone. 'I come here once a week to chill out and gather my thoughts.' Fuck! It was like looking in a mirror. A man who took time out to reflect on life. I prayed that he wasn't too good to be true.

'I've never met a man in a Jacuzzi before, certainly not a man who relaxes. All the men I've known are too hyper or immature to consider a day of relaxation.' I realised I'd informed him that I'd had a few men in my past.

'We're not all the same you know. Some of us are genuine.' He had to be my gift from the universe. I sent out a thank you. 'I've had a few disasters with women – it works both ways you know.' Mike gave me food for thought. I've known women who have cheated, lied and treated their other halves diabolically. I guess some men were victims of the torturous engagement of the single life too.

'Are you with anyone at the minute?' I asked. I needed to. Mike gave me a look of hope.

'I'm not with anybody at the minute. How about you?' His eyes burned into the depths of my soul. I'm sure it was the beating of my heart that caused the bubbling in the Jacuzzi. I responded in my usual tactful manner.

'I'm not with anybody either – too many dick heads out there.' Too far?

'Good to know, good to know.' Mike was looking into my eyes and I was wearing a bikini, which exposed seventy percent of my breasts. This was looking promising. Mike continued. 'Why are you still single?' I told myself to be honest.

'Well... basically, I've had no luck with men. I've met every type of arsehole there is. Not for the want of trying though.' Fuck it, I thought honesty was the best policy and a new trait for the new me. Mike articulated a pleasing smile and put his hands behind his head, pushing back his wet, dark rock style hair. His response startled me like no man has ever managed to do before.

'Sounds like my life story. I've dated lots of women with the hope of a serious commitment but I've been cheated on, used for money, lied to and nagged to bleeding death. There is no such thing as the perfect woman!' Mike spoke with conviction. I think I had met my match. I never considered the flip side to my manic disregard for the opposite sex. Mike had a soul, one similar to mine. I was hopeful that he wanted to see me again. I sent out plenty of thoughts for him to rip off my bikini right there, in the jacuzzi, but I think the universe would think that I was being too greedy and I would be punished for not being satisfied. I'm sure Mike could satisfy me – his biceps could easily throw me around the Jacuzzi. Nina used the analogy that men are sharks and if that is true then I'd just found myself a great white.

'Have you given up dating then, Mike?' I had nothing to lose by asking.

'No, I still live in hope but I'm happy to wait for the right woman to come along.' He was accurately like me. 'I'm staying here tonight. If you're not busy, you're welcome to join me for tea. If you don't have plans of course.' I was surprised that our views on love and life were similar. I had one more test. I stood up to leave the Jacuzzi.

'I'm going to sit in the steam room for a bit, you coming?' I walked past Mike and walked out on the steps of the Jacuzzi – I knew he would have to look at my scaly backside. He'd seen me without make up and knew my realistic views on life so I was willing to bare my flaws right there and then. I saw Mike's head turn as I reached the top of the steps.

'Nice ass.' Said Mike jovially. Jackpot! He wasn't a shallow human being who thought that a stretch mark was on the same scale as syphilis. I walked towards the steam room and Mike was right behind me. I'm not sure if he was going to be my Mr Right but I was sure he was bloody close to Mr Maybe.